What was s sh?

That was numb
interesting topi

Sunday morning, when she woke up in his arms, she'd figured out that she loved him. She hadn't wanted to leave his embrace. But she had—even though she'd had to work her anger to fever pitch to do it. Without that anger, she would have melted into his arms.

And now he was offering her a permanent place in his life. At least for a while.

But he wasn't offering love.

Which meant she couldn't ever be in his bed.

Could she live with the man and not plead for his touch? She didn't know. And that was what she would have to decide before she could give him an answer to his latest proposal....

Dear Reader,

Happy Valentine's Day! What better way to celebrate than with a Silhouette Romance novel? We're sweeter than chocolate—and less damaging to the hips! This month is filled with special treats just for you. LOVING THE BOSS, our six-book series about office romances that lead to happily ever after, continues with *The Night Before Baby* by Karen Rose Smith. In this sparkling story, an unforgettable one-night stand—during the company Christmas party!—leads to an unexpected pregnancy and a must-read marriage of convenience.

Teresa Southwick crafts an emotional BUNDLES OF JOY title, in which the forbidden man of her dreams becomes a pregnant woman's stand-in groom. Don't miss *A Vow, a Ring, a Baby Swing*. When a devil-may-care bachelor discovers he's a daddy, he offers the prim heroine a chance to hold a *Baby in Her Arms,* as Judy Christenberry's LUCKY CHARM SISTERS trilogy resumes.

Award-winning author Marie Ferrarella proves it's *Never Too Late for Love* as the bride's mother and the groom's widower father discover their children's wedding was just the beginning in this charming continuation of LIKE MOTHER, LIKE DAUGHTER. Beloved author Arlene James lends a traditional touch to Silhouette Romance's ongoing HE'S MY HERO promotion with *Mr. Right Next Door.* And FAMILY MATTERS spotlights new talent Elyssa Henry with her heartwarming debut, *A Family for the Sheriff.*

Treat yourself to each and every offering this month. And in future months, look for more of the stories you love…and the authors you cherish.

Enjoy!

Mary-Theresa Hussey

Mary-Theresa Hussey
Senior Editor, Silhouette Romance

Please address questions and book requests to:
Silhouette Reader Service
U.S.: 3010 Walden Ave., P.O. Box 1325, Buffalo, NY 14269
Canadian: P.O. Box 609, Fort Erie, Ont. L2A 5X3

JUDY
CHRISTENBERRY

BABY IN HER ARMS

Silhouette
R O M A N C E™
Published by Silhouette Books
America's Publisher of Contemporary Romance

SILHOUETTE BOOKS

ISBN 0-373-19350-5

BABY IN HER ARMS

Copyright © 1999 by Judy Christenberry

This edition published by arrangement with Harlequin Books S.A.

Printed in U.S.A.

Books by Judy Christenberry

Silhouette Romance

The Nine-Month Bride #1324
†*Marry Me, Kate* #1343
†*Baby in Her Arms* #1350

†Lucky Charm Sisters

JUDY CHRISTENBERRY

has been writing romances for fifteen years because she loves happy endings as much as her readers do. She's a bestselling writer for Harlequin American Romance, but she has a long love of traditional romances and is delighted to tell a story that brings those elements to the reader. Judy quit teaching French recently and devotes her time to writing. She hopes readers have as much fun reading her stories as she does writing them. She spends her spare time reading, watching her favorite sports teams and keeping track of her two daughters. Judy's a native Texan, living in Plano, a suburb of Dallas.

Chapter One

"Wahhhh!"

Josh McKinley stared down at the baby in the car seat next to him as if she were an alien newly arrived on earth.

"Listen," he began, desperation in his voice, "I know you're not happy, but I'm not, either. I mean, it's not that I don't—that is, I know you're—hell, I don't know what I'm trying to say."

A little sob was the only response. Not that he expected conversation from an eight-month-old, but he didn't have anyone else to talk to. And it made the baby stop crying.

At least, he'd thought it had. She'd apparently only been taking a breather so she could scream louder.

Nervously he leaned over and snapped on the radio. The hard rock he usually listened to didn't seem appropriate, and he scanned several stations until he found one playing a soothing melody.

Again the baby—his baby—stopped crying.

His baby.

When Child Protective Services had called his office earlier that day, he hadn't gotten back to them right away. He was busy. Besides, he didn't do kids.

Joshua McKinley, Private Investigator, was one of the top private eyes in Kansas City. He could pick and choose among the many cases offered.

They called back, leaving another message.

He'd had a client consultation that was tricky. He'd call them later. They probably only wanted a donation or something.

At five-thirty he had wrapped up the details of several cases and was chatting on the phone with a model he'd dated a time or two when call-waiting had interrupted. He'd almost ignored it. But the model seemed to have rocks in her head instead of brains. Besides, the call might have been a new case.

"Hello?"

"Is this Joshua McKinley?"

"Sure is. What can I do for you?"

"You could try returning your calls," the female voice had said indignantly.

"Who is this?"

"Abigail Cox, Child Protective Services. Didn't you get my messages?"

Even his mother hadn't chastised him as determinedly as this stranger. He'd straightened his shoulders. "Yes, I did, but I'm running a business here."

"And I have a very unhappy baby who needs her daddy."

"Lady, if the case isn't too complicated, I can take

it on, pro bono, in a couple of days. Send me the details.'' He wasn't an unfeeling monster.

"Mr. McKinley, it won't take the detective skills of Sherlock Holmes for you to find the baby's father. It's you.''

He'd opened his mouth, but no sound had come out. Taking the phone receiver away from his ear, he'd stared at it as if it had bitten him. Finally, he'd put it back to his ear. "What did you say?''

"Are you deaf as well as slow? I said—''

"Listen, lady, I don't have to listen to your insults, and I'm not—''

"You're right, and I offer my apologies. It's been a very frustrating day.''

He'd heard the weariness in her voice and figured he should cut the lady some slack. He knew he wouldn't want to deal with a bunch of kids, and the poor woman was going to have to face the fact that she'd made a mistake.

"Hey, you've got my sympathies. Hope you find the right guy.'' He was starting to hang up when she'd yelled loud enough to get his attention even though the phone was inches from his ear.

"Yeah?''

"Mr. McKinley, *you* are the right guy.''

Joshua was snapped back to the present by his companion in the darkened car. Obviously tired of the music, she drowned it out with her hysterical crying, distracting him from the review of earlier events.

"Baby, you can't do that,'' he muttered, grabbing his head with one hand. The pain between his eyes was growing unbearable.

Big blue eyes stared at him. Then the baby opened her mouth and screamed again.

Hell, what was he supposed to do? He knew nothing about babies. And it was a girl! Maybe if the baby had been a boy, he would have been able to figure things out. But a girl! The plumbing wasn't even the same, much less the emotions.

Desperately reviewing the females of his acquaintance, not for the first time, he shook his head in despair. His only family consisted of a distant cousin somewhere near Boston. He hadn't been seeing anyone regularly since Julie—and look what that had gotten him. He eyed the screaming baby with astonishment again.

He scanned the neighborhood as he drove, but he didn't expect an answer. The world seemed uncaring of his difficulties. Until he saw the illuminated sign of the Lucky Charm Diner.

Mike O'Connor!

Josh had done some work for Mike a couple of years ago, just before the man died. He'd had a couple of daughters, and Josh had discovered a third one Mike hadn't known about.

Kind of like *his* situation.

What were the daughters' names? Kathryn, Mary Margaret and…and Susan. Right.

He whipped his car into the parking lot. It was almost ten o'clock. If nothing else, he could buy some milk for the baby. And maybe some advice.

He'd take whatever he could get.

Mary Margaret O'Connor smiled. Kate was going to be so pleased. Not that Kate was dependent any longer on the diner or her catering company, since she'd married Will, but the more money the diner made, the more she would be able to help Susan.

Kate paid one-third of the profits from the diner to Susan, one-third to Maggie and kept one-third. After all, the diner was their father's legacy to them.

Dear Pop. He wouldn't even recognize the diner if he were alive. Kate had made it nouveau chic for the bluebloods of Kansas City.

Maggie's thoughts were interrupted by a noise that she at first mistook for a siren, but soon determined was a baby crying.

Here? This late at night?

Curiosity propelled her out of her chair. Grabbing her empty coffee cup as an excuse, Maggie left the small office behind the kitchen and pushed through the swinging doors into the restaurant.

There she stopped and stared at the handsome hunk who was holding a baby as if someone had just handed him a bowling ball that he didn't know what to do with.

"Glad you're here, Maggie," said Wanda, the night waitress, as Maggie entered the restaurant.

"What's up?" Maggie called over the screaming baby. Why didn't the man do something?

"This guy's looking for you or Kate." The waitress, tired and cranky, glared at him, then turned her back.

Maggie stared at him. What could he want with her? Suddenly wishing her big sister were here, she barely nodded at the man; he was handsome enough to leave any woman speechless, with his tight jeans, broad shoulders and bright blue eyes. Involuntarily, her insides turned to Jell-O.

"You're Mary Margaret? Mike O'Connor's daughter?"

"Maggie. I'm called Maggie." He probably hadn't come here with a screaming baby to find out her nickname.

"Maggie, I'm in trouble here."

She could tell that, in spite of the fact she knew little about babies. But what did he want from her? "Wh-what's the problem?"

To her shock, he shoved the baby toward her. Automatically she put out her arms and found herself holding the screaming baby. Then she jiggled the child gently and crooned to it, "Easy, sweetie, don't cry. It's okay, don't cry."

Immediately, the baby stopped crying.

A loud cheer went up from the few patrons.

The baby began screaming again.

The man spun around and glared at the customers, putting his finger to his well-shaped lips.

Though Maggie continued to try to soothe the baby, her gaze never left the man. He turned back to stare at Maggie, as the baby settled down again, a hopeful look on his face that made her nervous.

"Who are you?" she finally asked softly as the baby's eyes slowly closed.

"Josh McKinley."

Frantically she ran that name through her head and came up with nothing except a vague feeling that she'd heard it before. But where? Most of the men

she knew worked at the accounting firm where she
was employed. This man wasn't one of them. Not
with those muscles. She would've remembered.

"I'm sorry, I don't—"

"I'm a private investigator. I found your sister for
your father."

"Oh. Right. Pop mentioned—"

"I know you don't owe me anything, but I need a
woman."

Maggie felt her jaw drop, and she quickly snapped
her lips together. If someone had needed a woman,
an O'Connor woman, it had always been Kate, her
vibrant, red-haired sister. Not quiet Maggie.

"Why?" she whispered.

He stared back at her as if she'd just asked the
stupidest question in the world. "Why? The baby, of
course."

Maggie stared at the sleeping infant in her arms
and then back at him. "You're looking for a baby-
sitter? Why do you think I would know where to—"

"Not a sitter. At least—" He rubbed the back of
his neck. "I mean, I *will* need a sitter, I guess, but
right now, I need someone to tell me what to do."

Maggie kept thinking everything would become
clear if she asked a few questions, but each answer
was only muddying the water. "What to do about
what?"

She'd forgotten to whisper, and the baby's eyes
fluttered open and she began crying again.

"That!" he said in frustration.

Putting the baby on her shoulder and patting her
back, Maggie stared at him. "The baby?"

"Of course the baby! What else could I mean?"

Fed up with the going-nowhere conversation, she straightened her shoulders. "Look, Mr. McKinley, let's start at the beginning. Whose baby is this?"

"Mine." His single word seemed to come out reluctantly, and he looked away.

Maggie stared at him, blinking rapidly at the unexpected answer. "Yours? You're the father?"

"Yes, damn it!"

"What's her name?"

"How do you know it's a girl?" he demanded.

"She's wearing pink."

"Oh. Yeah."

"Her name?" Maggie prompted.

"It's— Damn, I can't remember!"

Maggie gasped as if he'd revealed a heinous crime. "You don't know your own daughter's name?"

His cheeks flushed. "I...I was in shock. You don't understand. I didn't even know about her until they...they handed her to me. I know they mentioned—" He rubbed his forehead. "It's an old-fashioned name. It'll come to me."

"I can't believe you don't know your—"

"Lady, cut me some slack! I told you—it's on the papers I have in the car." He turned to leave, and Maggie was filled with fear that he wouldn't return.

"Where are you going?"

He stared at her in surprise. "To the car to find out her name. That's what you wanted, wasn't it?"

"No! I mean...how do I know you'll come back?"

Her question didn't make him happy. That much was evident by his glowering face. Suddenly he reached into his back pocket and pulled out a thick wallet. "Here's my driver's license, my money and my credit cards. Okay?" He laid the wallet down on the counter and strode to the door.

Maggie stood there, holding the baby, staring at the wallet as if she feared it would try to get up and run away by itself.

Two minutes later he reappeared with a small bag. "Everything's in here," he muttered, digging around. Triumphantly he pulled out papers. "Virginia Lynn. That's her name, Virginia Lynn."

Maggie pulled the baby away from her shoulder. "Ginny? Is that your name, sweetheart?"

The child hiccuped, then reached for Maggie's dark hair.

"When was she last fed?"

"They gave her a bottle at four, because I hadn't called. I remember they told me four o'clock."

He acted as if he deserved a prize. "Okay, then she's probably hungry. What is she supposed to eat?" Maggie asked.

"Hell, lady, why are you asking me all these questions? I don't know anything about babies. That's why I need a woman."

Maggie let her lids settle gently over her eyes to hide herself from the angry man in front of her. But he didn't go away. She knew because she could hear his raspy breathing, as if he'd run a race…or was upset.

"Did they include anything in the bag?"

"The bottle's in here, but it's empty." He dug it out and handed it to her.

"Wanda?" she called over her shoulder. "Could you clean this bottle and fill it with milk?"

"Whole milk or skim?"

Maggie looked helplessly at Josh McKinley, and he shrugged his shoulders. She moved closer to hand him the baby.

He backed away. "Hell, lady, you aren't going to give up because I don't know what kind of milk, are you?"

Exasperated, she said, "No! But I thought you could hold the baby while I call my sister. My nephew is almost a year old. Kate will know what to do."

He reluctantly took the baby back into his arms, holding her against his body, as if he'd learned from watching Maggie.

She headed for the phone, and the baby started crying again.

"She hates me," he protested, following Maggie.

"Don't be silly. She's probably not used to a man's voice. Speak softly." She dialed Kate's number.

"Kate, do you know what kind of milk a baby should have?" she asked as soon as Kate answered.

"Maggie? What?" her sister asked.

"A man is here with a little baby, and we're fixing a bottle, but I don't know if she should have skim milk or whole milk."

"How old is she?"

Maggie hated to ask the man for more information, but she had no choice. Not that she expected him to know. "How old?"

To her surprise he said, "Eight months. She was born last October."

She repeated the information to Kate.

"Whole milk is fine. She can probably eat a little mashed potatoes, too, if they're not heavily seasoned. Now, tell me what's going on."

Maggie explained about Josh McKinley.

"Hey, maybe your sister could take her in tonight, just until I can arrange things," the man suggested.

Maggie suddenly realized he was standing right next to her, his shoulders brushing hers. "I doubt—"

"Ask her."

"Kate, he wants to know if you can take Ginny tonight."

"He what?" Kate squawked. "No, no, I can't. Nate has come down with the chicken pox from a child in his play group. I don't think it would be good to—"

"Oh, no. You're right."

"Look, I'll pay—" Josh urged.

"Her baby has the chicken pox," Maggie explained.

Before the man could respond, Ginny whimpered again.

Kate spoke before Maggie could. "You'd better get off the phone and feed her. And don't forget to change her diaper. She's probably wet."

Maggie hung up the phone. "Do you have any dry diapers? When did you last change her?"

"Change her?" Dawning realization stole over the man's handsome features. An unpleasant realization. "You mean—" He gestured to the baby's bottom.

"Of course that's what I mean. You haven't changed her, have you?" she asked as her own realization occurred. "How long have you had her?"

"A couple of hours. I couldn't figure out what to do."

"Do you have diapers?"

"You'll have to look," he insisted, clutching the baby against him with two hands, as if he feared she'd run away.

Maggie opened the bag and found five unused disposable diapers. "Good. I'll show you where you can change her while I fix some potatoes and her bottle."

"Potatoes?"

"My sister said she could eat them. This way."

"Wait a minute!" he gasped as he followed her. "I can't— I mean, I've never— You do it!"

"It's not difficult, Mr. McKinley. And she is *your* daughter." She wasn't about to admit that she wasn't very experienced in that area herself.

Gesturing to the sofa in her office, she turned and left the room, feeling guilty. She hoped poor Ginny didn't suffer from her father's lack of experience.

In the kitchen she heated up some mashed potatoes Kate had prepared before she'd left for the day. Wanda washed the bottle in silence, a sure sign that she was upset, and slapped it down on the counter beside the milk she was warming.

"There! It's clean. But I think you should throw the guy out on his ear. His story sounds pretty hokey to me."

"We really haven't even heard his story, Wanda, and the baby's so sweet."

"Hmmmp!" Wanda snorted and pushed through the swinging doors.

"She's changed," Josh said, stepping into the kitchen.

Maggie stared at the mangled diaper, its sticky tabs at strange angles. But at least the diaper wasn't falling off. "Good job." She could afford to be generous.

His sheepish look surprised her. "I had to throw away two others. Those sticky things got stuck on— on other things."

"Then your next stop had better be somewhere you can buy diapers. The two you have left won't last very long." She knew that much, at least. Kate was always complaining about the number of diapers Nathan used.

He looked panicky again, but as he drew closer to Maggie, Ginny gurgled and held out her hands, plainly asking Maggie to take her.

Maggie's heart flipped over and she grabbed the warm little body. "Oh, you sweetheart. Are you hungry?"

She held the baby in one arm and picked up the bowl of potatoes. "Fill the bottle with warm milk and bring it to me," she ordered, as if she cared for Ginny every day of the week, and sailed through the swinging doors.

Josh stared at Maggie's cute little backside as she swung away from him. Then he shook his head. He shouldn't even be noticing such a thing. He had a baby to care for.

Ginny. He had Ginny to care for.

And Ginny wanted Maggie.

He couldn't blame her, but he also couldn't deny the pang of jealousy that filled him.

Dismissing such silliness, he took the milk from the stove and filled the bottle, screwing on the nipple, and followed Maggie.

"Have you eaten?" Maggie asked as he slid into the booth across from her.

"Me?" It took time for him to remember. "Uh, no. I went to see about...about Ginny and—no."

"Wanda, bring Josh a menu," Maggie ordered, never lifting her gaze from Ginny.

Josh knew why. His child, little Ginny, suddenly seemed to have eight hands, waving and reaching, trying to catch hold of the spoon Maggie wielded.

Then he was distracted by the menu Wanda handed him. It took him no time to place his order, and the food was brought to him amazingly fast.

After shoveling food down with as many manners as he could summon, he leaned back against the seat and realized Maggie was holding his child, watching him in silence.

Ginny wasn't watching anyone. Snuggled against Maggie's neck, she slept peacefully.

Josh wasn't slow. He immediately realized what he needed. He asked Maggie the only possible question.

"Will you come home with me?"

Chapter Two

Quiet, shy Maggie O'Connor stared in disbelief at the handsome man opposite her.

His cheeks burned red and he hurriedly added, "I mean, for Ginny. Come home with me to help out with Ginny."

Still, she could say nothing. Words wouldn't come to her.

"I promise I don't mean anything else. No...no playing around. I mean, your dad trusted me. You can, too." He was getting his embarrassment under control, she could tell, since the red in his cheeks began to disappear.

If only she were as quick to recover. "I...I don't think—"

"Think about Ginny. I don't know how to care for her. Every time I touch her, she cries. Her mama just died and—"

Those words got Maggie's attention. "Her mother just died?"

"Yeah, so—"

"You don't seem very broken up about it!" She couldn't keep the accusatory tones out of her voice. Having lost both of her parents, Maggie took death seriously.

She expected a quick show of sorrow, a repentant attitude. Instead she discovered frustration when she looked at him.

"I'm not exactly celebrating," he said grimly, "but I hadn't seen Julie in almost a year and a half. She never even told me about Ginny. It wasn't until today that I learned of her death and Ginny's existence. I've been hit kind of hard."

Maggie turned her head to stare at the baby, whose warm little body pressed against Maggie. Sympathy welled up in her for the orphan. Her own mother had died at Maggie's birth. She and Ginny had a lot in common, because the child would never remember the mother who'd given her life, just as Maggie didn't.

"What are you going to do?" she asked.

"I'm still hoping you'll come home with me."

She studied him under lowered lashes. He was a sexy, handsome man. A lot of women wouldn't question his intentions if he asked them to come home with him. They'd even be disappointed if he expressed disinterest. Maggie, however, wasn't surprised by his promise that he didn't mean anything sexual with his offer.

Kate said she gave off the wrong vibes to single

men. Maggie didn't know if that was true, but she'd found it easier to deal with numbers than real live men. Ginny, however, was another story.

"Where do you live?"

He sat up straighter, a spark of hope lighting his eyes. "I have a condo a few blocks from here, near the Plaza."

His private investigator business must be successful, Maggie realized, since that was a pricey neighborhood. "Even if I take care of Ginny tonight, that's only going to delay your problem twenty-four hours."

"One Day at a Time. That's my motto." He sent her a smile that she figured usually got him whatever he wanted from a woman.

"Why did you take her?"

He looked like she'd thrown a glass of cold water in his face. "What?"

"I said—"

"I heard you. Because I'm her father."

"Are you sure?"

"Why are you asking these questions? What difference does it make to you? I asked you to help care for her for twenty-four hours, not write a biography."

Maggie stiffened, causing Ginny to shift. "It seems to me that you should be more agreeable if I'm supposed to do you a favor."

"Ah. We're wanting to know how much I'll offer? Is that it?"

Enraged, Maggie slid from the booth. "Here, Mr. McKinley, take your baby and leave. I don't need insults." Though she tried to hide how reluctant she was to let Ginny go to her father, she bent toward the man so she could hold on to the soft bundle of joy a little longer.

"Wait!" he protested, panic in his eyes. "I didn't mean to insult you. And you'd be doing me a huge favor. I don't mind paying."

"I don't think I asked for any money."

"Maggie, please help me, just until tomorrow."

She hadn't intended to agree to his crazy plan. After all, she didn't know him. Her father may have trusted him with a few family secrets, but he hadn't said he'd hand over one of his daughters to him for repayment.

But Maggie had no fear that he would be interested in her. And she had a lot of fear about what would happen to Ginny. Not that she herself knew all that much about babies, but she knew a little. She'd taken care of Nathan on occasion.

"Please?" His blue eyes, exactly like Ginny's she suddenly realized, pleaded along with his word.

"I...I suppose I could help you out tonight. I'll take Ginny home with me and you can pick her up in the morning." She cuddled the sleeping baby against her again, aware of how happy she was to do so.

"No!"

Maggie blinked at the man as he jumped to his feet, crowding her in the aisle.

"But you said—"

"I asked you to help me, not take my baby away."

"But I can't spend the night at your place. That would—"

"That would be best," he hurriedly said. "I prom-

ise I won't touch you. Ginny needs to get used to her
new home.''

She tried to picture what it would be like to stay
in the same apartment as Josh McKinley. He probably
had a bachelor pad, completely inappropriate for a
baby. "I don't think that's a good idea.''

"You're not taking Ginny some other place. She
stays with me. But I could use your help.''

Ginny smacked her rosebud lips, as if still taking
the bottle, and Maggie's heart swelled with love.
She'd heard of falling in love at first glance, but she
hadn't expected the recipient of her emotions to be a
baby. "All right. I'll help you out until morning. I go
to work at seven-thirty.''

"Maggie, you're the best!'' he exclaimed, smiling
that sexy smile again. "Are you ready to go? We
need to buy some diapers and some milk before we
go home.''

Josh couldn't believe his luck. He'd convinced
Maggie to come home with him and take care of
Ginny.

They'd moved the baby seat to the back and Maggie had strapped Ginny in without waking her. Then
they'd driven to one of the few all-night groceries.
Josh knew its location because he usually shopped at
odd hours.

Maggie had remained in the car while he'd pur-
chased only the necessities. Then they headed toward
his apartment.

"I hope you don't mind not going to your place.
But it'd take an hour to go to North Kansas City and

back. I bought you a toothbrush.'' He glanced her way, not sure what kind of response he was looking for.

"Thank you. I'll pay you back as soon as we get the baby settled.''

Her cool tones told him he hadn't been forgiven for the things he'd said earlier. "Come on, Maggie. I didn't mean to insult you. I apologized.''

"Yes, of course. I'll still pay you for the toothbrush.''

He grinned. "I should've known you'd be stubborn. After all, you're Irish, just like your father.''

She didn't respond to his smile. "I'm not like my father.''

Even as he mentally made a note of her response, he muttered, "You could've fooled me.''

Nothing else was said until he wheeled his car into his parking space in the garage attached to his building.

"If you'll get Ginny, I'll bring everything else.'' There were two suitcases Child Protective Services had given him, as well as the grocery bag.

As their small procession made its way to the door leading to his condo, Josh realized his life had changed. This morning he'd had no idea he had a daughter.

Yep, everything had changed. But he wasn't going to let it affect him.

Maggie marched along, still disturbed both by Josh's attempt to pay her and her acceptance of his plea for help. She'd never spent the night with a man, even as a baby-sitter. She couldn't help being nervous.

When Josh told her they'd arrived, setting down the suitcases and juggling the grocery sack to find his keys, she suddenly wondered what she'd find in his apartment. She'd always heard bachelors were messy. After all, she'd seen *Animal House*. When he pushed the door open and gestured for her to precede him, she prepared herself for anything.

To her surprise, she discovered a spacious, comfortable living room, with only a few items out of place. "How nice."

"What did you expect? A hovel?" he asked, grinning again.

"No, but I'd heard—that is, some men aren't neat."

"Don't go putting a halo on my head, Maggie. I have a cleaning woman who comes in every week. She was just here yesterday."

"Oh. Well, it's still nice. I like the colors." The room was mostly done in masculine colors—forest green and tan.

With a nod, he started down the hall. "You and Ginny can sleep in my bed. Bring her this way."

"But she can't sleep in a regular bed. She'll turn over and fall off," Maggie protested. At least she knew that much about babies.

"She can turn over?" Josh asked, staring at his daughter as if he expected her to perform the miracle right now.

"Yes. They start turning over when they're about four months. Ginny can probably crawl, too.

"What are we going to do? I don't have a crib."
He stood there, his hands on his hips, a puzzled look
on his face.

Maggie fought the urge to put her arms around him.
He looked so concerned for his baby. In fact, in spite
of all the questions in her head, she had to give Josh
credit. For a tough guy, he was being remarkably sen-
sitive to his baby girl's needs.

"Maybe we can put pillows around her, build a
barrier so she can't fall off before one of us notices."

"Good idea. Thank God you came with me, Maggie. I wouldn't have managed without you."

Maggie savored his words as she followed him into
his bedroom. The king-size bed would provide plenty
of room for her and Ginny, that was for sure. "Do
you have another bed? Where are you going to
sleep?"

"The other bedroom is a home office, right now.
I'll take the couch." He busied himself lining up the
back of a chair next to the bedside table. "I'll get the
other chair from my office."

Maggie laid Ginny down on the bed and checked
her diaper. Just as she'd expected. The baby needed
another change. She unfastened the sleeper, taking the
little feet from their warm pockets.

"What are you doing?" Josh gasped over her
shoulder.

Maggie jumped, unprepared for his sudden return.
"I—I'm changing her diaper. She's wet."

"Again? Already?"

"Babies are like that. Would you bring me a clean

diaper?'' She wasn't sure where he'd left the bag he'd had earlier or the grocery sack.

Without a word he hurried out, returning quickly with a clean disposable diaper. ''Aren't you afraid she'll wake up?''

''I think she'll sleep through the change,'' Maggie whispered. ''All that crying wears a baby out.''

''I'm glad it's good for something,'' he muttered, returning to his construction of a barrier on the other side of the bed.

''Does she have any clean clothes in those bags? She rubbed mashed potatoes into this outfit.''

''I'll get the suitcases.''

Inside the bags, they discovered numerous articles of clothing and several stuffed toys. Maggie couldn't help thinking about the woman who'd given birth to this darling baby and bought so many things for her. ''Her mother certainly provided well for her.''

''Yeah...except for a daddy.''

She had no answer for his response. Selecting an adorable pink nightgown, she gently dressed the sleeping baby, only rousing her slightly before Ginny settled back into sleep.

''I can't believe she's sleeping so soundly,'' Josh said in a whisper.

Maggie smiled but said nothing. Josh had lined the side of the bed with chairs and a long king-size pillow. She felt sure Ginny would be safe. She pulled back the cover with one hand before settling the baby on the mattress, breathing a sigh of relief when a tiny snore signaled Ginny continued to sleep.

Maggie slipped carefully off the bed and stood there, staring at the baby.

"She's beautiful, isn't she?" Josh murmured.

"That wasn't your attitude when you arrived at the diner," she reminded him with a weary smile.

"Babies don't look so good when they're screaming." He continued to stand there. Finally he said softly, "Do you think she'll ever get used to me? Like me?"

The warm feelings that rushed through Maggie scared her. They almost overwhelmed her intentions to keep her distance from Josh McKinley. But in spite of her warnings to herself, she couldn't help but reassure him. "Of course she will. Little girls always love their daddies."

"Did you love yours?"

"Of course I did!" She stared at him, wide-eyed, wondering what could've made him think she didn't love her father.

"You seemed upset when I said you were like him."

"Not upset. But Pop often said I was a changeling, unlike him and Kate." She dismissed the silly pain that that thought always caused her. "I think I'll get ready for bed. I usually get up at seven, but I'll need to make it six-thirty so I can go home and change." She paused and stared at the sleeping baby. "I hope I'll know if Ginny needs help. I'm a very deep sleeper."

Josh grinned at her. "I believe she'll let you know. After being the recipient of her screams most of the evening, I'm an expert on how loud she can be."

"I hope so," Maggie agreed, but knowing her own ability to sleep through alarms, she still worried.

"I'll get you a T-shirt to wear," he said, acting as if he had complete faith in her. He took a T-shirt out of the dresser and then went back to the living room to get the toothbrush he'd bought her.

After taking it from him and saying good-night, Maggie went to the master bath and prepared for bed, even taking a quick shower with her long brown hair pinned up on top. She washed out her underwear and hung it on the towel rack. Then, dressed in his shirt which came almost to her knees, she opened the bathroom door and peeked out.

Josh wasn't in sight. She hurried over to the bed and slid beneath the covers. Just as her head hit the pillows, there was a knock on the door.

"Yes?" she called softly, her heart thudding.

"Do you need anything?" he asked through the door.

"No. We're fine." Or she would be if she could forget that Josh McKinley was sleeping in the next room. Had he forgotten his pajamas? Was that why he'd come to the door?

She almost asked if he needed to get anything before common sense warned her to say nothing. She didn't think Josh McKinley looked like a pajamas kind of guy.

Great. Thinking about what he slept in wasn't going to make it easier to get to sleep.

Josh called a soft good-night, and Maggie turned on her side and thumped the pillow. But several minutes of peace and quiet, broken only by the even breathing of the baby beside her, and, contrary to her expectations, Maggie drifted off to sleep.

A sudden ringing jerked Maggie from a deep slumber. She reached toward the sound and lifted the telephone receiver. ''Hello?'' she muttered, her head falling back onto the pillow.

She almost drifted back to sleep because no one said anything. Then a rough voice asked, ''Where's Mac?''

''I don't know,'' she muttered, and started to hang up the phone when the bedroom door opened.

''Maggie? Was that the phone?''

Why was a man in her bedroom? She stared at the shadowy figure, confused. ''They want Mac.''

''That's me.'' He crossed to the side of the bed and took the phone from her. ''Mac, here.''

Maggie let her eyes close, ignoring the conversation next to her. She wanted to go back to sleep.

''Damn! I'll be right there.''

Blessed silence and she'd almost lost consciousness when that sexy voice intruded again. ''Maggie, I have to go. I'll be back as soon as I can.''

''Umm-hmm.'' The door closed again and she was in total darkness. Sleep claimed her.

''Ba-ba-ba-ba-ba!''

Maggie rolled over. What a strange night. First she'd dreamed there was a man in her bedroom, and now someone—or something—was babbling.... Maggie sat bolt upright. The baby!

''Oh, Ginny, are you all right?''

The baby was lying on her tummy, drool running down her little chin, and she actually smiled at Maggie. Suddenly the day seemed brighter.

"I guess you are. Though I'd bet you're ready for a diaper change and some breakfast. I'll just have enough time to take care of those things if we hurry. Then your daddy can manage. I hope."

Maggie slid from the bed and dashed into the bathroom to gather the slacks, shirt and underwear she'd worn last night. She'd have to change while watching Ginny to make sure the baby didn't fall off the bed.

Once she was dressed, Maggie picked up the baby and opened the bedroom door. "Maybe we should be quiet in case your daddy is still sleeping," she said softly.

Tiptoeing into the living room, Maggie came to an abrupt halt when she discovered the sofa vacant. Ginny, unaware of Josh's absence, began to whimper, distracting Maggie from her discovery.

She located the diapers and returned to the bedroom, snatching up a clean sleeper from the suitcase. As she quickly changed the baby, she tried to figure out where Josh was. Maybe he'd gone out to get a paper. Or bagels? Her stomach rumbled at the thought. Or maybe he was in the hall bathroom. She hadn't heard the water running, but then she was concentrating on Ginny.

"There, now you feel better, don't you, sweet girl? Let's go scramble you some eggs for breakfast."

She surreptitiously checked the hall bathroom on the way to the kitchen, but it was empty. No one in the kitchen, either. How was she going to scramble eggs and hold Ginny at the same time?

Returning to the suitcases in the bedroom, she found a large baby blanket. Pulling the comforter off the bed, she folded it several times and put it on the floor in the living room and spread the baby blanket over it. She put Ginny in the center of it with one of her stuffed animals. The baby seemed content.

Maggie hurried to the kitchen. She might not be the cook her sister was, but she could scramble eggs. Only a couple of minutes later she carried a saucer of scrambled eggs and a hastily refilled bottle to Ginny.

Two hours after that, with Ginny contentedly playing, Maggie sat rigidly on the sofa, staring at the morning news on the television. She'd turned the TV on to see if Josh McKinley had made the headlines overnight. He hadn't come back from any of the places she'd imagined he'd gone.

Then, as she waited, vague memories of a phone call in the night came to her. And Josh telling her he'd return as soon as possible. She wondered just how long that could be.

Because *she* had to go to work. She'd been with the accounting firm of Jones, Kemper & Jones ever since she'd graduated from college four years ago. And she'd never missed a day of work.

But today she'd had to call in sick. She figured Josh McKinley would be on TV news tonight because either he'd been the victim of a violent crime, or she was going to kill him when he walked through the door.

Chapter Three

It wasn't until Josh emerged into the sunshine at about ten o'clock that morning that he remembered Ginny...and Maggie O'Connor.

And suddenly he was reminded why he'd never considered remarrying and having children.

"Damn," he muttered beneath his breath.

The man beside him, the one who'd called him in the middle of the night, his best employee, Pete, asked, "What's wrong?"

"Nothing."

"You sure it doesn't have anything to do with the sexy lady who answered your phone at three in the morning?"

"I guess that's why you're so good at your job, Pete. You figure things out." He shrugged his shoulders, trying to dismiss any concern.

"Don't worry, boss. She'll come back. You know

this P.I. stuff makes them think you're a combination of Superman and Dick Tracy.''

Josh stared at his employee as if seeing him for the first time. ''And you play it for all it's worth?''

Pete must've picked up on Josh's tone of voice, because his own grew more serious. ''Only if it's what they want. You know how women are.''

He'd thought he did. But somehow he didn't think a certain lady was going to accept his occupation as a reason to abandon his child. What was he going to do?

''Do we have anything else that can't wait?'' Josh asked, his lack of sleep finally hitting him.

''I don't think so. Want me and Don to handle things for a day or two?''

''Yeah. Take some time off today to catch up on your sleep, but tell Sharon not to call me unless its unavoidable. I've got some things to do.''

''Right, boss.''

Josh strode toward his four-wheel-drive vehicle, feeling about ninety years old. He used to be able to pull an all-nighter without a problem. Was he getting too old at age thirty-three? Pete was only about five years younger.

No, it must be the worry about Maggie and Ginny. He already knew what Maggie's reaction would be. He'd seen his mother limit his father's life because she wanted him to conform to her rules.

His father had been a fireman, dedicated to his job. He'd finally given it up when Josh was ten, selling insurance for a living the rest of his life.

And as unhappy as any man could be.

Josh had married when he was twenty-four. He'd thought he was in love. But he made sure he explained his work and why he wouldn't give it up. Six months later he'd walked out because she insisted he go to work for her father.

No way, no how.

Then he'd met Julie, Ginny's mom. She hadn't liked his job, either. But he'd explained his terms. They'd rocked along for almost a year. Until they both realized the other was convenient for good sex and a fun date—but nothing more.

She'd left, and she hadn't bothered to tell him about Ginny.

Sliding behind the wheel, he sighed. What was he going to do? As Maggie had pointed out, he had to make some decisions, not just about today but long-term.

But first he had to face Maggie.

When he walked into the apartment, Maggie was on the phone and Ginny wasn't in sight.

"I'll be over in a little while, Kate. Mr. McKinley just arrived."

Josh winced as she hung up the phone. Her sarcastic tone confirmed what he'd expected.

"Sorry, Maggie."

"How interesting," she said coolly. "You say that as if you expect your apology to be enough." She folded her arms over her nicely shaped chest and glared at him.

"I say that because I don't know what else to say."

She didn't respond. He guessed Pete was wrong.

Being a private investigator wasn't winning him many points.

"Look, Maggie, it was an important case for my best client. There was a man who was about to get away with a lot of money."

"And Ginny? What if I hadn't been here?"

It struck Josh that she hadn't complained for herself. Only for his child. And she had a valid point.

"I don't know."

"Josh, a baby can't be—"

He lifted his lids, trying to stave off sleep, wondering why she'd stopped.

"You haven't had any sleep, have you?"

He shook his head. Frowning, he looked around again. "Where's Ginny?"

"In bed, taking a nap. I suggest you join her."

A miracle. He'd discovered a woman who knew what he needed. With a thankful smile, he struggled to his feet and headed to the bedroom. Then he came to an abrupt halt.

She'd also gotten up. And picked up her purse.

"Where are you going?"

"Home. If I hurry, I can change and make it to the office for a half day of work."

All thought of sleep left him. "No! You can't go! I need you."

"Mr. McKinley, in spite of your lack of sleep, I think you'll have to admit I kept my promise. I told you I had to leave at seven-thirty. It's now ten-thirty. Enough is enough."

His tired brain wasn't functioning at top speed. "But—but what if she wakes up?"

"You change her diaper, feed her and cuddle her. It's simple." She started toward the door.

He might be tired, but he could still run. He beat her to the door, leaning against it, making it impossible for her to leave. "Maggie, just a few hours more."

"I can't believe you have the nerve to—"

He held up his hands. "I know. You've been more than generous. But as soon as I get some sleep, I need to go shopping for all the things she'll need. And I don't even know what she can eat. Just help me with those things. Please, Maggie? I'm more than willing to pay you for your time."

Maggie stared at the man in front of her. The dark circles under his eyes and the slump of his shoulders pleaded for her to be understanding, even more than his words. Josh McKinley had had a rough night.

But Maggie believed that as long as she was his crutch, he would never deal with his baby girl. He wouldn't change his life to include Ginny.

"Josh," she began, reverting to his first name instead of the more formal Mr. McKinley, "you can't stash a baby somewhere and then disappear. You're going to have to change your life."

"I will, I promise, Maggie, but give me today. You've already missed half a day. What's another half? I bet you seldom miss work."

Maggie could have told him she *never* missed work, but Kate had assured her that wasn't always an admirable trait. And he was right. Her perfect attendance record was gone, whether she missed a half day or the rest of the year.

Trying to ignore the relief that was flooding through her, she said, "All right. I'll stay and help you shop. While you sleep, I'll make a list."

To her surprise, he leaned forward and cupped her face in one of his large hands, placing a kiss on her cheek. "Thanks, Maggie. You're a doll."

Then he stumbled into the bedroom, softly closing the door behind him.

Maggie stood there, staring at the space Josh had occupied, touching her cheek. She was staying for Ginny. She told herself she needed to repeat those words over and over again.

Until she forgot the excitement that had filled her at his touch.

Until she dismissed his words and the yearning to believe them.

Until she remembered she was just Maggie.

"Josh, you've already bought a bed, a playpen and a high chair. Do you really think you need to buy a swimming pool?" Maggie asked in disbelief.

"But she enjoyed her bath so much, Maggie," Josh observed. "Don't you think she'd like this little swimming pool?"

Maggie stared at the stranger in front of her. Gone was the private investigator. In his place was a doting father. As long as he didn't have to hold his baby.

Every time she'd suggested he hold the baby, he'd had a reason not to. He'd watched Maggie bathe Ginny, chuckling over Ginny's enthusiastic splashing.

He'd fixed another bottle for her, but he'd insisted Maggie should feed her.

Now he was willing to buy almost anything and everything in the store.

"No swimming pool. You don't have room for it." She pushed the buggy down the aisle.

"How about a stroller?"

Maggie turned around and found Josh had only moved a couple of feet and was studying some very elaborate strollers.

"Josh, we have to finish. I still have a long drive home, and we haven't been grocery shopping yet."

She'd intentionally mentioned her going home. Josh had sworn he only needed her to help with the shopping. She needed to keep reminding them both of that.

When he'd pleaded with her to stay, she'd been honest enough to admit to herself that she was relieved. Ginny was firmly wrapped around her heart.

And that was the main reason she had to go.

"You're right, Maggie. We've certainly taken advantage of your good nature." He accompanied his charming words with an even more charming smile.

She returned his smile, careful to hide the disappointment inside her. Disappointment? She should be thrilled to return to her own life.

"I found a big book about babies on the other aisle. I think I'll add it to our purchases. Then I can study up on what to do."

"You can always call me if...if you have a question. I'll leave my number for you." The only problem would be whether she knew the answer. Her own experience was limited to taking care of her nephew, Nathan, for an hour or two at a time. But somehow she couldn't face losing touch with Ginny and her sexy daddy.

"That's very nice of you."

Maggie knew it wasn't niceness that had prompted her words.

"Will you watch her while I go find that book?"

"Of course." Replaced by a book. That didn't say much for her mothering skills, did it? Maggie turned to the gurgling baby, sitting in the baby seat in the buggy, her heart lifting at the happy sound. "We haven't done so badly, so far, though, have we Ginny?" she said softly.

When Josh returned with the aforementioned book, he added it to the pile of purchases. "Can you think of anything else we need?"

"No, Josh. I think you've bought enough things for ten babies."

"Gosh, I hope I don't get any more," he said, eyes wide. "It's a frightening thought, that I might have more babies out there that I don't know about." He moved ahead of the buggy, hooking his finger in the front of it and pulling it toward a checker. "Come on. Let's get out of here."

Maggie didn't argue. Lifting Ginny out of the seat, she cuddled the baby against her. The approaching departure, leaving Josh and Ginny on their own, already hurt. But she had no place in their lives. Better to leave now, while she could survive, than to hang around until he didn't need her anymore.

Josh got one of the stock boys to help him load all

their purchases in the back of his Jeep Cherokee. Maggie strapped Ginny in her car seat, handing her a rattle Josh had insisted she needed.

"Here, sweetheart. Enjoy."

After a kiss on Ginny's chubby little cheek, Maggie got in the front seat and fastened her seat belt. She watched out of the corner of her eye as Josh did the same.

He said nothing until they reached the grocery store. Then, however, he reached over and caught Maggie's arm as she started to get out.

"Wait. I just want to tell you again how much I appreciate all you've done for me…and Ginny. I don't know how I would've managed without you."

His words were sweet. His touch took her breath away.

"It was nothing."

"It was a lot, to trust me like you did."

She shrugged her shoulders. "I'd be glad to take care of Ginny a little longer if I didn't have to work."

"Like you said, that would solve my problem for one night, but I've got to make some long-term changes." He frowned. "I'm just not sure exactly what they are."

"You'll need to find a nanny. Someone who will live in, to cover for you when you have to go out late. There are agencies you can call."

"How soon do you think they'll be able to find someone? I mean, I'll take off work, but emergencies happen."

Maggie's pulse sped up. She stopped to consider before she spoke. After all, she'd never been impulsive. But the past twenty-four hours with Josh and Ginny had been more exciting and pleasurable than any in the past year. For that matter, years.

She'd hidden from life most of her existence. But her father's death had taught her an important lesson. Life offered no guarantees. She'd promised herself she would learn to live it more joyfully. But all she'd done was follow the same routine she'd established long ago.

Her father would've hated such cowardice.

"Why don't I stay with you until Monday? I'm sure they can find someone for you by then."

Josh stared at her. "Are you serious? You would do that?"

He seemed almost as surprised as Maggie was at her offer. She shrugged her shoulders. "I've got a lot of vacation time due to me, and I've fallen in love with Ginny. She's such a sweetheart."

"If you're sure, Maggie, I'll accept your offer. And I owe you big-time."

With the lightness that filled Maggie's heart, she wondered if perhaps she might be the one owing him.

Maggie had insisted on driving her car back to his condo after their trip to her apartment. Josh had followed her, not liking the idea of her driving after dark alone. She'd laughed at his concern. But he'd followed her anyway.

Panic filled him every time he thought about the changes he was going to have to make in his life. But he would make them. He didn't shirk his responsibilities.

Tomorrow morning he was going to start calling

agencies and find a nanny. That's what he needed. A twenty-four-hour nanny.

One just like Maggie.

After they got back from the drive to her apartment, he spent the evening putting together the crib, the high chair and the playpen, leaving Maggie to deal with Ginny.

She was a beautiful baby. But he wasn't going to fall into the trap of having to give up the job he loved, like his father had. And he feared time spent with Ginny would trap him.

Maggie and Ginny appeared in the door of his second bedroom, now in total disarray with the desk shoved back against the bookcase to leave room for the newest purchases.

"Are you ready for Ginny to go to bed? She's getting sleepy."

"Uh, yeah. I just finished with the high chair. I'll take it to the kitchen."

"Aren't you going to kiss Ginny good-night?"

"I'll make her cry."

"I don't think so. She's getting used to you." Maggie moved closer.

He stepped back. "She'll cry."

"Ginny, don't you want your daddy to kiss you good-night?"

He knew Ginny couldn't understand what Maggie had said, but the baby nestled against Maggie's shoulder and gave him a sleepy smile.

"See? She wants her good-night kiss."

Cornered, Josh leaned over and touched Ginny's

cheek with his lips. Baby powder and baby sweetness were heady scents. Josh stepped back at once.

Maggie had washed the new baby sheets and put them on the bed. She laid Ginny down and wound up the mobile they'd bought that hung over the baby. Ginny's eyes widened, and she kicked her little legs.

"I think she likes it," Maggie whispered. Then she touched Josh's arm, urging him from the room.

Picking up the high chair, he headed for the kitchen. Anything to get away from the emotions tugging on his heart. When he turned around, he discovered Maggie hadn't followed him.

Had she decided to turn in? It was almost ten. Maybe she wanted to avoid conversation with him. It had been a while since he'd shared living quarters with a woman. He'd forgotten how to adapt.

The dishes from dinner were soaking in the sink. With a weary sigh, Josh began loading the dishwasher. Mrs. Lassiter wouldn't be back for five more days. Too long to leave the dishes.

"I think I'll turn in now, Josh, if you don't mind."

He whirled around, almost dropping the glass he'd been rinsing.

Maggie stood there in a cotton robe, her face scrubbed clean, her hair hanging loose to her shoulders. She looked almost as innocent as Ginny, and he felt a protective tenderness toward her, as well as a disconcerting desire.

"Sure. I imagine you're tired."

"No more than you. Change is hard to handle."

He cleared his throat. "Uh, yeah." Having Maggie around was almost as unsettling as having Ginny.

She waited, as if she thought he would say something else, but he didn't know what to say.

"Good night," she finally said and walked out of the kitchen.

He fought the urge to follow her, to assure her everything would be all right. But he didn't because he didn't know if it was true. He didn't know what he was going to do about Ginny. She was his responsibility. And he would ensure she was well provided for. But how?

He doggedly rinsed the dishes, staying away from the bedroom. That was dangerous territory. When he'd finished washing up, he wiped his hands and decided he'd best make up the sofa for another uncomfortable night. The damned thing wasn't long enough for his body.

He walked past the living room door before he realized what he'd seen. Turning around, he crossed the distance to the sofa quickly.

"What are you doing?"

Maggie, wrapped in a sheet, her head on a pillow, opened her eyes and stared up at him. "I thought you were a private investigator. You need me to tell you I'm trying to sleep?"

"You're supposed to be in the bedroom."

"Why?"

"Because you're my guest. You're doing me a favor. Now, come on."

He turned to precede her, then realized she hadn't moved. In fact, she'd shut her eyes.

"Maggie!"

She shifted on the sofa, and his gaze immediately

traced her body beneath the covering. Unbidden came the question of what she wore to bed. Her cotton robe hadn't given any hint.

"Maggie, come on. I really want you to sleep in the bed."

"I'm comfortable, Josh. And the couch isn't big enough for you."

"I'll manage."

She closed her eyes, completely ignoring him.

He squatted down to look her in the eye—if she would only open them. "Do I have to carry you to bed?"

He hadn't realized how suggestive his words were until heat flooded his body. And her cheeks.

Her eyes flew open. "You do, and you'll be taking care of your baby by yourself."

"Hey, no fair," Josh protested. "You know I need you to stay."

"So I'm staying. Go away and let me sleep." She closed her eyes again.

He stared at her serene face, her dark lashes long against her delicate cheeks. Maggie was so different from any other woman he'd ever known.

Unable to stop himself, he reached out and ran a finger down her cheek. Her skin was petal soft, and he felt a tightness in his groin.

She jerked, her eyes widening in shock. "What…what are you doing?"

"Trying to convince you to get a good night's sleep," he whispered, working hard to keep his hands off her. Her velvety skin drew him.

"I'll get a good night's sleep if you'll go to bed and leave me alone." She closed her eyes again.

"We could share." Maggie wasn't like the women he dated. She wasn't overtly sexy. She didn't flirt. He knew she'd be shocked by his words. But he found the thought of taking her to his bed a pleasurable one.

She didn't even open her eyes. "Go away, Josh, or I'm leaving."

He stood. This time she had the upper hand.

It wouldn't last.

Chapter Four

When Maggie awoke the next morning, the apartment was quiet. She hurriedly dressed in jeans and a shirt she'd brought from her apartment.

Today was Friday. She'd take today off from work as a vacation day, and she'd promise to be in early Monday morning. Her employers wouldn't like it, but they had no choice. She had a lot of vacation days saved.

As she waited for the coffee to perk, she heard Ginny talking. Hurrying down the hall, she quietly opened the door to the second bedroom.

Ginny saw her at once and beamed. With an answering smile on her face, Maggie crossed to the crib. "Good morning, Ginny. Do you like your new bed?"

"Ma-ma," Ginny cooed, reaching her arms up for Maggie.

"Oh, sweetheart, no! My name is Maggie." She

repeated her name several times, but the baby kept saying "Mama."

After changing Ginny's diaper and dressing her in a playsuit, Maggie took her to the kitchen. Carefully following the instructions about Ginny's schedule on the pages she'd found in the suitcase last night, Maggie fed the child her cereal and juice.

After breakfast Maggie carried Ginny to the playpen set up in the living room and set her down in it with several toys. "Time for me to clean up your mess, little one."

When she'd finished tidying up, Maggie wondered what she was supposed to do with herself now. Realizing that she needed to do whatever she could to resolve the situation she was in—before she broke her heart—she picked up the Yellow Pages of the telephone directory.

Half an hour later she had a comprehensive list of agencies that provided child care workers. But since she didn't know Josh's financial situation, she couldn't select one in his price range. He'd certainly spent money freely last night, but that didn't mean he could afford a pricey nanny.

Checking her watch, she realized it was eight-thirty. With a determination belied by her trembling fingers, she pushed up from the sofa and headed for the master bedroom.

Knocking on the door, she waited for an answer. Nothing. Finally she turned the knob and opened the door. "Josh?"

His back was to the door as he lay sprawled on the bed, and he didn't move.

"Josh?" When he didn't respond, she approached the bed and shook his bare shoulder.

He sprang into action, grabbing hold of her wrist and pulling. Maggie screamed as she hit the bed.

Josh hadn't slept so soundly in a long time. Nor had he awakened so swiftly. Suddenly he was in the middle of his king-size bed with Maggie sprawled on top of him, a frightened look on her face.

"Maggie? Are you all right? What's wrong? Where's Ginny?"

"You're...you're naked!" Maggie said with a gasp, her big hazel eyes staring at his chest.

He looked down at himself, puzzled. "No, I'm wearing shorts," he assured her, but he didn't understand why his attire was being discussed.

She tugged at her wrist, and he realized he was holding her. He turned her loose—reluctantly he noticed—as she scrambled from the bed.

"You didn't answer my questions. Is everything all right?"

"No! I wanted to awaken you, not do hand-to-hand combat!" she protested, straightening her shirt.

He looked at the clock. "I didn't realize it was so late. Sorry. But you took the day off from work, didn't you?"

"Yes, but not so you could sleep in."

Righteous anger filled her voice, and he couldn't resist teasing her. Lifting the covers slightly, he said, "There's room for you, if you're jealous."

With a look of disgust, and maybe just a hint of

temptation—at least he hoped so—she turned around and slammed out of his bedroom.

He chuckled until he thought he heard another door slam. He sprang from the bed, afraid she was leaving. "Maggie? Maggie, you didn't leave, did you? I was just teasing."

His only answer was Ginny's babbling.

Panicking, he ran down the hall. "Maggie? Maggie?"

"For heaven's sake, put on some clothes," she said crossly, looking away when she realized he hadn't dressed.

The sight of her sitting on the sofa, her arms crossed over her chest, filled him with relief. Though he'd appeared in front of other women with less apparel than he was wearing now, Josh hurriedly backed out of the room.

"I'll be right back," he promised as he returned to his room to dress.

Maggie felt like a prim old maid. Why hadn't she acted more composed? Her behavior had all but told Josh she was inexperienced. In fact, she could've worn a sign on her forehead that said "Virgin" and not been as obvious.

After giving Ginny a kiss on her soft baby curls, Maggie hurried to the kitchen. Not that Josh deserved breakfast, but it would give her something to do. Hopefully, it would also make their next meeting less tense.

She was scrambling eggs to accompany the bacon and toast when Josh appeared in the doorway. Maggie felt her heart race in the presence of his rugged masculinity.

"Maggie, you didn't have to cook for me," he said as he entered the kitchen.

"It doesn't matter. Did you check on Ginny?"

"She's fallen asleep. Is that normal?"

She glanced at his concerned frown before turning away. "The notes say she takes a short nap every morning." After setting a full plate on the breakfast table, she crossed to the kitchen counter to get him a cup of coffee.

When she turned, she was surprised to discover Josh standing right behind her. The coffee sloshed over the side of the cup, and she gasped as she set down the mug. He grabbed her hand and turned on the cold water at the sink.

"Don't move until the burning stops. I'll get a towel."

She drew in air as he moved away from her. The man affected her breathing more than a five-mile run. Before she could compose herself, he was back at her side.

"How does it feel now?" he asked, indicating her hand.

"Fine," she assured him as she pulled away. "The burning's stopped." And it had, because the coffee wasn't that hot. But even if it had scalded her, she couldn't have remained that close to Josh.

"Sit down and I'll pour you a cup."

"I've already had two cups. I don't think—"

"Some juice, then. I'll pour you some juice."

He seemed intent on keeping her at the table with

him, but she was just as determined to put some distance between them. He wasn't showing much skin now, but even in his tight jeans and a knit shirt that molded his muscular chest, he was more than she could handle.

"No, I need to check on Ginny."

"She's asleep, Maggie. Sit down."

Having run out of excuses, she collapsed in the seat across from him. He poured a glass of orange juice and put it down in front of her before taking his own place, coffee cup in hand.

"The breakfast looks great," he said, smiling.

"Good."

"It's a real luxury to have someone else do the cooking. Thanks."

She kept her gaze on the glass of juice. "Welcome."

Tense silence filled the small kitchen as he took several bites of bacon and egg. From under downcast lashes, Maggie watched as he lowered his fork to his plate. A quick glance told her he still had a good deal of breakfast to eat.

"Maggie, I'm sorry I embarrassed you. I was afraid you'd left."

"It's all right," she said hurriedly, looking longingly toward the door. "I overreacted."

"I'm sorry I slept late, too. I don't usually. I shouldn't have stayed in bed so long," he added.

Josh's voice was calm, comforting, but when he extended his hand across the table toward her, she jumped back.

He sighed. "Maggie, you're acting like a cat on a

hot griddle. Did I frighten you so very much this morning?''

"No, of course not. I'm just not used to— I live alone.'' Stupid response. She tried again. ''I mean, I don't usually wrestle with anyone before I— Well, most people don't wake up like you.''

He grinned. ''Sorry, old habit.''

It was time to change the subject. ''I made a list of agencies for you to call about a nanny. But I want to alert you that some of them may be very expensive.''

Her warning didn't seem to bother him. ''That was good of you. I suppose I'd better start calling.''

She nodded, breathing a sigh of relief when he stood. Yes, it would be good when Josh lined up someone else to take care of Ginny. Because it was time she returned to her solitary apartment. Before it became too difficult to leave.

She rose to clear the table as Josh headed for the living room, only then realizing he hadn't finished his breakfast. ''Josh? Don't you want any more breakfast?''

''Huh? Oh, I forgot.'' He appeared as distracted as she did. Which made her feel better.

''I'll...I'll go check on Ginny.'' She sped from the kitchen before he could protest.

Josh watched Maggie flee the kitchen as if she were being pursued. Glumly he turned his attention to his breakfast.

He made her uncomfortable.

Hell, she made *him* uncomfortable. He wasn't sure

why. She wasn't unattractive, if a man liked the quiet type. Her brown hair was lustrous, silky, but it was brown, not blond, his usual choice.

She didn't flirt with him. In fact, she avoided his touch whenever she could. Instead of agreeing with him, she argued and tried to tell him what to do. Of course, he needed her to do that when it came to Ginny.

But he didn't need to want her. She was definitely off limits, because she was a homebody. One who would want her husband home every evening, mowing the grass every weekend. Selling insurance, or doing some other deadly dull job.

Having finished his breakfast, he took the dishes to the sink, rinsed them out and put them in the dishwasher. Then he walked to the living room, his resistance in good shape.

Only to discover Maggie and his daughter cuddling on the sofa, Ginny giving fat chuckles as Maggie teased her chin.

"Having fun, are we?" he asked, unable to resist smiling, too.

"Yes. Why don't you hold her? She's in a very good mood."

Maggie's suggestion stopped him in his tracks. "No, uh, I'd better not. Where is the list you made? I need to arrange for a nanny right away. We've taken advantage of you more than we should have."

She pointed to a piece of paper on the plank coffee table.

He settled into his favorite leather chair beside the lamp table that held the phone and made his first call.

Half an hour later he hung up in frustration. "I can't believe it. They charge outrageous fees and won't work a minute past five o'clock. No weekends. Eight o'clock is their starting time and they expect you to provide everything."

He didn't get much sympathy from Maggie, who was still playing with Ginny. "Child care is always expensive."

"I don't mind the expense, but I don't work an eight-to-five job. And I'm not going to give it up." He realized he was clenching his teeth and that Maggie was staring at him.

"You'll have to have someone who lives in."

"I tried that. The only two I could find insisted a two-bedroom condo wasn't large enough to accommodate them. They wouldn't share a room with Ginny."

"Maybe you could find a small house."

"I don't want a small house. I like it here!" he insisted, challenging Maggie with his stare.

Ginny whimpered and buried her face in Maggie's hair. She immediately turned her attention to the child. Josh didn't like being ignored, but it gave him time to compose himself. After all, Maggie hadn't asked him to make changes. The circumstances were demanding it.

"I guess what you really need is a wife," she said as she soothed the baby, still not looking at him.

"No! A wife expects too much. The only way I could marry would be as a…a business agreement." He'd spoken from the heart, but considered his words with his mind. "Hey, that's not a bad idea. A marriage of convenience. I could find someone who needed a place to live and—"

The phone rang.

"Yeah?" Josh listened as one of his commercial clients gave him directions for an emergency trip he needed Josh to take. He completely forgot about the two females on the sofa as he grabbed a pen and made notes. "Right. I'll have him there."

He leaped from his chair and headed for the bedroom to grab a jacket and some spare money.

"Where are you going?"

He came to an abrupt halt. "Damn! Maggie, I have to go. I don't have anyone else to do this job. Both my guys are already on assignment."

Silently she stared at him, her hazel eyes large.

"Look, I'll be back this afternoon, late. I have to pick up a witness. It's just a couple hours' drive. I'll take the guy to court and come straight back here. No later than three or four, I promise."

"I don't know, Kate. Actually, I'm getting a little worried. He said he'd be back by three or four and it's almost seven now."

"He's taking advantage of you, Maggie," Maggie's sister Kate protested over the phone. "Just because he did a job for Pop doesn't mean you owe him anything."

"I know. But I volunteered, and Ginny is such a sweetheart." Maggie paused, trying to think of a way to explain to her sister. "If it were Nate, would you want me to abandon him?"

"Of course not, honey, but you worry me. You've

always cleaned up my messes when you should've let me suffer the consequences.''

''You didn't complain when Sister Mary Agnes couldn't figure out who'd papered the convent when I swore you were with me.''

Kate chuckled. ''I know. You were so saintly, she couldn't believe you'd lie.''

''She was always too harsh in her punishment, or I would've told on you myself.''

Kate chuckled again. ''Don't give me that tough talk. I know how soft your heart is.''

''Yeah, I guess so,'' Maggie agreed with a sigh. ''But Kate, Ginny really needs me. She…she calls me Mama.''

''Oh, Maggie, see, that's what I mean. You're not her mama and it's going to hurt when you have to leave her. I don't want you hurt.''

''This may be my only chance to be called Mama.'' That was the core of Maggie's heartache. She wanted a family, a child. But she never attracted men, or, for that matter, met men other than those she worked with. And she would never date someone in her own office.

''That's a ridiculous statement,'' Kate protested.

Maggie could hear her sister's famous temper in her words. When Kate was riled, it was best to stay out of her way. ''Now, Kate, I'm just facing facts.''

''If you're ready to change your life, I'll introduce you to some men. There are lots of executives in Will's company. I'm sure—''

''You'll find someone who will marry the boss's sister-in-law as a favor? No thanks.''

"Maggie! Why do you say things like that? I'm sure any number of men would fall in love with you on sight if you'd just let them."

Maggie had long ago accepted that she was not as beautiful as Kate. She chuckled. "Yeah, it's hard to walk because so many of them are prostrated on the floor around me. Come on, Kate. I'm not you."

"Of course you're not. You're better. You're sane, rational, careful—"

"All sexy things that attract men."

"Maggie, you're not being reasonable."

"I know. How's Susan?"

The change of subject frustrated Kate, Maggie could tell by her huffing and puffing, but she couldn't resist talking about the young woman who they'd recently discovered was their sister.

"She's doing okay. Her sister graduates from high school at the end of the month. I thought we should all go out to eat together to celebrate. I want to find the right present. Want to go shopping with me?"

"Sure, as soon as Ginny's settled. Did you give Susan her rightful share of the profits from the diner?"

Kate chuckled. "Yes, and she had the nerve to grill me about whether I was padding the profits to help her out."

Susan was a proud young woman, determined to manage to raise her half siblings by herself. Kate and Maggie had to work to get her to accept anything from them. "I wonder where she gets her hardheadedness from?" Maggie teased.

"Probably from you, sister, dear. Or I suppose we

can ultimately blame Pop, since he passed his stubbornness to all of us.''

''Not me. Pop always said I was the changeling because I didn't have red hair, remember?'' Maggie reminded her.

''Oh, Maggie, that was a silly joke. Of course you take after Pop.''

Maggie didn't have a comeback for her sister's obvious lie. Ginny saved her, however. ''I hear Ginny awakening, so I'll have to go,'' she told Kate.

''All right, but if that Josh doesn't show up soon, you call me. And when he does show up, I think you should walk out and leave him to clean up his own messes.''

Maggie gave a noncommittal response and hung up the phone. After spending almost forty-eight hours with baby Ginny, she knew she couldn't walk away from the infant unless she knew Ginny would be well cared for.

''Here I am, sweet girl,'' she called out as she reached Ginny's room. The baby had pulled herself to her feet and was holding on to the top rail of the crib, tears glistening on her cheeks and a smile on her face.

''You are so adorable,'' Maggie whispered as she picked up the baby and cuddled her against her chest. ''And wet. Oh, my, looks like we have to change again. I think it's time for your bath now.''

She rounded up everything necessary for the bath and soon had Ginny sitting in the kitchen sink, splattering water everywhere.

''I wish your daddy was here. He likes to watch

you bathe.'' She poured a little baby shampoo in her hands and cleaned Ginny's curls. After she rinsed the baby's head, with some protesting on Ginny's part, Maggie lifted her from the sink and wrapped her in a baby towel.

"In fact, my angel, I think your daddy loves you a lot. But for some reason he's afraid to admit it. So the next time he comes close to you, I want you to reach out for him. Okay? Show your daddy that you love him.''

She wished she could count on Ginny understanding. So far the baby had reached out to her over and over again, but Josh was another story.

"Maybe it's because he's not around that much.''

She carried the baby back to the second bedroom, dried, powdered and diapered her, then dressed her, inhaling her delicate clean-baby scent with satisfaction.

Back in the kitchen, Maggie put Ginny in the high chair, adding a bib in a vain attempt to keep her clothes clean. "I'm a little worried about your daddy. He hasn't called or anything. I know he has an unpredictable job, but you'd think he'd remember he has a baby depending on him.''

She'd almost finished feeding Ginny when she heard a noise in the hallway. Was that Josh coming home? It was almost seven-thirty.

She stepped to the kitchen doorway just as the outer door swung open and a bloody figure stumbled through.

Chapter Five

"Josh!" Maggie screamed.

Josh slumped against the wall. "Look, Maggie, I know I'm late, but I can explain."

"What happened to you?"

"Shh," he said, holding a finger to his lips. Then he motioned for the man with him to enter the apartment. The witness Josh had set out to collect this morning, Sam Ankara, didn't make a sound, but his gaze focused on Maggie.

Maggie, looking sane and normal, if a little disoriented, was a welcome sight to both men. Josh closed the door and locked it. Then he sat down beside the phone and dialed a number, holding up a finger to Maggie as she started to ask a question.

"Don? I need back-up. At my place. Right away." After he hung up the phone, he looked at Maggie's big hazel eyes, which were filled with concern. "I know I said I'd be back by three or four, but we ran into a few delays along the way."

"Why do you have a bandage on your head? And blood on your shirt?" she demanded. Before he could answer, Ginny let out a shriek from the kitchen. Maggie ran from the room, but almost before Josh could relax against the leather chair, she returned, with Ginny in her arms.

"Well?" she asked.

"I was shot at. Sam, sit down, try to relax."

"I don't understand," Maggie protested as the other man crossed the room and collapsed on the sofa.

"Sam, here, is an important witness in my client's case. Someone doesn't want him to testify."

Maggie sank down on the wooden chair by the wall as Ginny batted her cheek with a pudgy baby hand. "You mean—someone tried to kill you?"

"Not me. Sam. I just got in the way."

"Have you seen a doctor?"

"Yeah, I've seen a doctor, and the police. Everything's taken care of." Well, except for one or two things, but he didn't want to mention them to Maggie right now.

"Have you eaten anything? There's not a lot here, but—"

"We're starving." He looked at her hopefully. "And Don probably will be, too."

Instead of heading to the kitchen, Maggie walked over to his side and picked up the phone. She dialed a number by memory and ordered four dinners, to be delivered. Hanging up the phone, she smiled at Josh,

a smile that was half demure and half wicked.
"That's going to cost you."

"What did you just do?"

"I ordered our dinner from Lucky Charm catering.
It will be here in half an hour."

He looked from her to the phone and back again.
"You can do that?" As she nodded, he asked, "The
pot roast I ate the other night?"

Again she nodded.

"You're brilliant! Sam, you're in for a great
meal."

Maggie had expected Josh to be irritated that she'd
handled the meal crisis by ordering in. But she wasn't
going to be his servant. She was there for Ginny. Besides, she wasn't much better as a cook than she was
a nursemaid.

Moving back to the chair by the wall, she allowed
her gaze to travel to the stranger sitting on the sofa.
He looked decent enough, but he was pale. Of course,
knowing someone wanted you dead would be a little
off-putting.

"What did the police say?" she asked.

"Duck faster," Josh assured her cavalierly.

"Josh! That's no answer. Are you out of danger
now?"

"As long as we don't show our faces in public,
sure."

"Won't they follow you here?"

"No!" the man on the sofa protested. "They
won't, will they, Josh? You said I'd be safe here."

"We weren't followed," Josh said, shooting a warning glare in Maggie's direction.

Maggie got the message, but she had a few more questions, mostly about logistics. "So, in the morning, you'll go to the trial and—"

"No. Today is Friday, remember? The trial won't resume until Monday morning."

Josh's quiet response left Maggie with more questions than ever. "So Mr.— I'm sorry, I didn't catch your name."

"Sam Ankara. I'm an accountant."

Maggie smiled. "So am I."

Josh appeared startled, and Maggie realized they'd never spoken of her job. As she and Sam chatted about the problems in their line of work, Sam actually began to relax.

Finally Maggie turned back to Josh to discover he was leaning against the back of the chair, his eyes closed. "Um, Josh? Where is Sam going to stay? I mean, have you made him a hotel reservation?"

"He's going to stay here," Josh said without opening his eyes. "He'll have to sleep on the sofa."

"But wouldn't he be more comfortable in a—"

"I can't guarantee his safety in a hotel."

"I won't be any trouble, Mrs. McKinley. I'll even help with the baby. I have three kids of my own." The man's earnest assurance, and the huge misconception that inspired it, left Maggie speechless.

Even Josh opened his eyes. But if Maggie expected him to contradict Sam, she was mistaken. He closed his eyes again and muttered, "Good."

"Josh, could I see you in the bedroom, please?"

Maggie snapped. She smiled at Sam, not wanting him to feel unwelcome. "If you'll excuse us just a moment, something came up today that I need to discuss with Josh. There's coffee brewed in the kitchen if you'd like some before dinner arrives."

Still carrying Ginny, Maggie marched down the hallway. The baby rubbed her eyes with her fist, distracting Maggie from her intent.

"Oh, poor baby Ginny. It's your bedtime, isn't it? Josh, I need to put Ginny to bed first. Wait for me." After looking over her shoulder to see him nod, she turned right into Ginny's bedroom.

After changing another diaper and dressing Ginny in a nightie, she kissed the baby and tucked her into bed, turning on the musical mobile above her. "Night-night, Ginny."

Leaving the baby's room, Maggie stood in the hall a moment to gather her anger. Then she swung open the bedroom door without knocking, prepared to blast Josh McKinley out of his complaisance.

Only to find him asleep on the bed.

The bandage on the side of his head stood out even in the shadowy light of the bedroom. Probably he needed to rest. But Maggie couldn't figure out what he intended to do. There was only this one bed and the couch in the living room. And she had no intention of sharing with either man.

Of course! She would take the sofa. The two men could share the king-size bed. With that settled in her mind, she returned to the living room and Sam Ankara.

* * *

"Josh?"

The soft voice scarcely intruded into his dreams. After all, he'd been hearing that voice murmuring sweet things ever since he lay down. "Come on, baby."

"Josh! The food's here."

"Food?" That didn't fit into his dreams.

"Yes, the food I ordered. I think you should wake up and eat. Besides, your assistant, Don, is at the door. At least that's who he said he was. I didn't think I should open the door until you checked him out."

That information brought Josh awake. "No! You're right. I'm coming."

As he followed her from the bedroom to the living room, a thought struck him. "You let a deliveryman in?"

"Yes, of course."

"Maggie, you shouldn't have opened the door. It could've been anyone."

"I looked. It was Joey."

Without replying, Josh strode to the door. Through the peephole, he discovered Don and quickly opened the door, let in his assistant and relocked the door immediately.

"You weren't followed?"

"No. I was careful."

"Sam, this is Don Nichols, one of my best operatives. Sam Ankara, our witness. And—this is Maggie." Josh didn't know how to introduce her. He didn't see any point in telling Sam or Don that Maggie wasn't his wife.

Don nodded to Maggie, but Josh noticed his gaze lingering on her.

He cleared his throat. "We have a few problems to deal with. Maggie, would you look in the desk drawer in Ginny's room and get some pens and paper?"

"Certainly. But why don't you pass out the dinners and fix everyone something to drink while I do? We don't want the food to get cold."

The aroma of roast beef was assailing his nostrils and he hurriedly did as Maggie suggested. Maybe he'd feel better with some solid food in him, Josh reflected. Right now he couldn't seem to get his thoughts off Maggie.

The food was as good as he remembered, and by the time Maggie returned, half Josh's meal was gone.

"You like the dinner?" she asked, a smile on her lips.

Don and Sam both assured her of the food's perfection. Josh nodded. Then he motioned for Maggie to join him on the sofa, where her food awaited her along with a cup of coffee.

"I can eat in the kitchen if you need privacy to talk," she offered.

"No!" all three men responded in chorus.

"We're not going to be saying anything you can't hear," Josh assured her. "Where's Ginny?"

"Don't you remember? I put her to bed when you lay down."

"How you feelin', boss?" Don asked. "Your appetite seems to be okay."

"I was starving. My head aches a little, but not bad."

"What are we going to do now?"

"I'm going to keep Sam here for the weekend. My place is easy to guard. Besides, I don't think they'll try anything until we move him. It's easier that way."

"Okay. What do I do?"

Maggie watched Josh's employee. He seemed a little hard-edged but nevertheless friendly.

"I need you to go purchase a few items, then take up guard duty in the hallway. Since my apartment is the only one after the corner, we can stop anyone coming in. Get Pete to relieve you whenever you need it, and plan on doing that all weekend."

"Okay. Make me a list, and as soon as I finish, I'll do the shopping."

"Maggie, can you make a list for the grocery store?" he said, glancing her way. He didn't know whether she would protest being pressed into domestic duty or not.

She gave him a considering look, and he didn't know what to expect. Finally she said, "I'll fix breakfast and make sandwiches for lunch, and we can order in from the Lucky Charm for dinner. Is that okay?"

"Sounds good to me. Gentlemen, you won't mind eating dinners like this one, will you?" he asked, knowing the food was incredibly good.

Both Don and Sam murmured their agreement.

"Then we're set. Come Monday, our problems will be over." There were, however, a couple of sticky points between now and Monday morning, Josh thought grimly. Like how they would get Sam safely to the courtroom. And where everyone was going to sleep.

He shot Maggie a wary look, but she was carrying her dishes to the kitchen and didn't notice. Now that everyone seemed to think she was his wife, he figured they'd better share the bedroom. Better her than Sam for a roommate.

He only hoped she felt the same way.

Don returned with a toothbrush and several items of clothing for Sam, who had gone into the hall bath to wash up.

"Wouldn't it be easier for him to use the master bath with you?" Maggie asked. "After all, he'll be sleeping there."

"Where?" Josh snapped, staring at her.

"In the bedroom with you, of course. I'll take the sofa."

"No, you won't."

Maggie stared at him. "Why not?"

"You'll be in the bedroom with me."

She leaped to her feet. "I will not."

He stood, towering over her. He was a big man, and something about his size set her pulse racing. "Honey, you have to. Sam believes you're my wife."

"Then tell him I'm not." She raised her chin and stared back.

"I don't think that's a good idea. I don't know Sam very well. You'll be safer with me."

She wasn't ready to buy that excuse. "If he's with you, he can't be with me. Problem solved."

"I may sleep very soundly tonight. The doctor

gave me some pills. So I might not hear you if you called for me. It'll be better if we're together. It's a big bed, Maggie. I'm not going to attack you. I won't be up to it.''

''What kind of pills?'' She remembered when Kate had broken her arm because of one of her adventures. Maggie had had to wake her sister up several times during the night to be sure she was okay.

''Pain pills.''

''For a head injury? Are you sure he knows what he's doing? Did he caution you about waking up every four hours or something?''

He smiled. ''Yeah. He said to have someone check on me a couple of times during the night. See, if you share the bed with me, you can do that without disturbing anyone else.''

He seemed suspiciously cheerful to Maggie's way of thinking. ''You promise you won't— I mean—''

''I promise,'' Josh hurriedly said as the bathroom door opened. ''You'd better get some bedding for Sam.''

Maggie did as he asked, but she wasn't sure she'd made the right decision in giving in to Josh's plan. Somehow, sharing the bed with Josh held a lot more danger for her than the possibility of someone shooting at Sam.

After she'd given the linens to Sam, Maggie excused herself. While Josh talked to Sam, she moved her belongings from Ginny's bedroom to Josh's. That action alone seemed dangerous.

''You're being ridiculous!'' she told herself. ''Josh promised not to touch you.''

She believed he was a man who kept his promises. She'd realized that about him, if nothing else. But what about her? That question shocked her. Of course she wouldn't be interested in—in anything.

She hurried into the shower, then slipped on her cotton pajamas and robe. When she opened the bedroom door, she discovered Josh sitting on the edge of the bed, as if he were waiting for her.

"I thought I'd take a shower, if you're finished," he said, as if sharing his bedroom with a woman was a common occurrence.

It probably was.

That depressing thought kept her from speaking. She nodded and stepped past him, stowing away her dirty clothes as he entered the bath.

As soon as the door closed behind him, Maggie stared at the big bed. It was plenty big for two people. But she'd feel better if there was some barrier to ensure that they didn't touch.

Hurriedly, with anxious glances over her shoulder toward the bathroom, she took the king-size pillows and lined them down the center of the bed, underneath the covers. She'd already found some smaller pillows in the top of Josh's closet, one of which she'd taken to Sam.

Now she took two of those pillows and put them at the head of the bed. Then she stood back to survey her handiwork. With a nod of satisfaction, she slipped under the cover on the right side of the bed. After all, Ginny might wake up during the night.

When the bathroom door opened, Maggie tensed. Would Josh complain?

"You're on my side of the bed," he said gruffly, standing at the foot of it.

"But I'll need to get up if Ginny cries." She deliberately didn't look in his direction, in case he didn't wear pajamas to bed.

"I'm wearing my pj bottoms," he said, as if he'd read her mind.

She couldn't keep from looking then. The striped-cotton bottoms did cover him from the waist down. But his broad, muscled chest, flat stomach and wide shoulders were all bare. She gulped. "I...I appreciate that." Then she closed her eyes.

With a heavy sigh, as if she'd disappointed him, he rounded the bed and got in beneath the covers. Immediately Maggie felt too warm. Of course, she told herself, it could have something to do with the fact that she still wore her robe over her pajamas.

"Are you wearing your robe?" Josh asked. Again Maggie wondered if he could read her mind. That possibility sent fear shivering through her.

"Yes. I...I was a little cold."

"Take it off, Maggie. You can't sleep like that all night." With an edge of irritation, he added, "I gave you my promise."

After a moment of hesitation, she undid her robe and slid it off, tossing the garment on the foot of the bed. "Did you take your pill?" she remembered to ask.

"Damn, I forgot. It will probably be all right."

"No, Josh, you need to take it. Where are the pills? I'll get them."

"No, you won't. They're in the living room, where

Sam is sleeping. I'll get them." He shoved back the covers and got out of bed.

Maggie toyed with the idea that he'd almost sounded protective, even jealous, though she knew it was silly to think that even for a minute. Still it was…rather nice.

Damn woman was driving him batty, Josh thought as he entered the living room where Sam was lying on the couch reading.

"I forgot my pills," Josh muttered, snatching them off the lamp table.

"Glad you remembered. You probably wouldn't get much sleep without them. I've had a head injury before."

"Yeah. Night." He didn't want to talk to Sam Ankara. And he certainly didn't want to discuss the possibility of getting any sleep tonight.

Sharing the bed with Maggie was going to preclude sleeping. Why was she so sexy in her white cotton pajamas and robe? He'd had women in slinky black teddies come on to him. Or wearing nothing at all.

But Maggie, with her solemn hazel eyes and demure smile, was becoming more and more important to him. And sexier. But he'd promised to keep his hands to himself. And that explained why he wouldn't get any sleep.

Unless these pills were knock-outs.

He opened the bedroom door, then closed it behind him.

"Do you need water to take them?" Maggie's quiet, husky voice asked in the darkness.

"Yeah." He sensed movement from the direction of the bed. "I'll get it. Stay in bed." Those words sounded so familiar, so…hopeful. As though he was going to join her there.

And he was. But there was a big pillow separating them. He wasn't going to be able to touch her. He'd been angry when he'd first seen those pillows. Then he realized he should probably be grateful.

He didn't trust himself.

He slammed the empty glass down on the bathroom counter and turned off the light. Then he crossed over to the bed and got back in.

"Is your head hurting?" she whispered.

"A little. But the pill should fix it up. Good night, Maggie."

"Good night, Josh."

Whispered words in a darkened bedroom.

They should have been the prelude to something incredible.

Instead, they opened the door to torture.

Josh sighed and rolled over.

Chapter Six

Maggie had set the timer on her wristwatch to awaken her after four hours. When the buzzer sounded, she automatically switched it off as her mind tried to figure out why she would set the alarm while it was still dark.

Then she remembered Josh.

Which was a good thing, or she might've wondered whose arms were around her.

Arms? Suddenly, she was wide awake and sitting upright. Where was the pillow?

"Josh? Josh, what happened to the pillow?"

He stirred. "What?"

"Josh, I'm waking you up to see if you're all right. And to find out what happened to the pillow." And to try to forget the coziness she'd dispelled when she'd sat up.

"You need a pillow?" Josh asked, sounding confused.

"The pillow I used to…to divide the bed. Remember?"

"Come back to bed, honey," he said, his words slightly slurred. "We'll find it tomorrow."

A big warm hand tugged on her arm, and she almost did as he asked without thinking. Or because she'd liked sleeping in his arms.

"Uh, I need to check on Ginny." Anything to get out of that bed. She shoved back the covers and distanced herself from the temptation of his arms.

The apartment was quiet as she slipped into Ginny's room. The baby was sleeping on her tummy, her diapered bottom stuck up in the air.

Maggie tugged the blanket farther over her. Ever since she'd been with Ginny, the baby had slept until six in the morning. Three more hours before this special little alarm clock went off.

So there was nothing to keep Maggie from returning to the warm, maybe even hot, bed next door. What was she going to do?

Find the pillow, she decided. If she put the pillow back in place, everything would be all right.

With a sigh, she left Ginny's room and crossed the hall. Josh was asleep, sprawled on his stomach, just like Ginny. Maggie turned on the bathroom light after first pulling the door almost closed. A thin sliver of light shone into the bedroom.

Aha! There on the floor by Josh's side of the bed was one of the long pillows. She realized the other was at the foot of the bed, pushed out of the way.

She carried the pillow she'd found on the floor to her side of the bed. Josh was taking up more than half of the space, but he was a big man. She wouldn't fuss about that. Shoving the pillow toward the center, where Josh's arm lay, she hurried back to turn off the light, then got into her side of the bed.

Just as she settled down, she felt Josh shift, and she held her breath.

"Okay?" he muttered.

"Yes," she replied, keeping her voice soft.

When he said nothing else, she let her breath out slowly, allowing the languorous warmth to steal over her. Such a comfortable bed.

Just as she was drifting off to sleep, she vaguely noted movement from somewhere. Then strong, warm arms nestled her against a furnace. Such a comfortable, warm bed....

Maggie was dreaming about being toasty warm on a tropical beach, wrapped in the arms of a handsome man, when she heard Ginny's cries. Alarms always interrupted the best dreams, she thought ruefully.

As she struggled to open her eyes, the strong, warm arms of her dream tightened around her. That brought her awake.

"Josh!" she protested, her voice rough with sleep.

"Hmmm?"

"What happened to the pillow?"

"You asked me that earlier. You got a fetish about pillows?" he asked drowsily.

She sat up, pulling down her pajama top, which had somehow been shoved up, exposing her middle. "You—it's over there, again," she said, seeing the big pillow on the floor where she'd found it last night.

"The baby's crying," he reminded her. "Shouldn't you do something?"

That did it! She folded her arms and glared at him. "No, *I* shouldn't. She's your baby. *You* do something."

Her suggestion, or maybe she should call it a challenge, brought those sleepy bedroom eyes wide open.

"What? You want me to—but I don't know anything about babies. And I make her cry."

Maggie felt the urge to rescue the little girl from her father's inexperienced hands, but she fought it back. "I don't know much more than you. And you have to learn sometime. Besides, she's already crying."

"Come on, Maggie, you know she wants you," he pleaded. The bedroom eyes were now forcing all their seductive charm on her.

"She wants a dry diaper and a bottle of milk. You can figure out how to change a diaper, and the milk is ready in the refrigerator," Maggie said crisply. Then, doubling the pillow behind her, she leaned back against it and stared at him determinedly. He could be as charming as he pleased; she would resist to the end.

Josh recognized an intractable object when he saw one. And Maggie O'Connor, looking sexier than she should in her cotton pajamas, her crossed arms pushing her breasts toward the closure of her top, was intractable.

At least he'd gotten away without having to account for removing the pillow. The first time, he'd thrown the pillow aside in his sleep. When she'd awakened him, he'd been as surprised as she was to discover his arms wrapped around her. But the second time, he'd given in to temptation, remembering how good she felt against him. He'd wanted her back in his arms.

Not that he would've taken advantage of her or anything. He just wanted to hold her, like a kid with his favorite teddy bear. After all, he'd been injured—surely he was entitled to a little comfort?

He grinned as he stepped into Ginny's room. He didn't think Maggie would accept that argument.

"Hi, baby," he said softly, greeting his daughter. Several tears slowly ran down her little cheeks, but she smiled when she saw him.

"Willing to take any port in a storm, huh? Listen, we have to manage without Maggie just for this morning. She's in a little snit, okay? So be patient."

He grabbed a clean diaper and approached the baby's crib. He'd seen Maggie do this job several times, and he'd even managed it once at the diner. Not as efficiently as Maggie, of course, but he *could* do it.

"Time to change the diaper, sweetheart. Let's lie down," he said as he put her on her back.

Her big blue eyes widened and stayed glued to his face, as if she was trying to decide whether or not to cry. He reached up and wound the music on the mobile, making the animals that dangled down circle the crib.

As he watched Ginny's attention transfer to the animals, he decided changing a diaper wasn't so bad.

Even one that smelled a little. He didn't remember such a smell before.

Unsnapping her nightgown, wet from Ginny's long sleep and subsequent action, he noticed the smell seemed to get worse.

Uh-oh.

Pulling the diaper away from her skin, he peeked inside.

"Maggie!" he roared.

Maggie had been congratulating herself on forcing Josh to take care of Ginny, when she heard that desperate roar. Fearing something terrible had happened to the baby—which, of course, would be Maggie's fault—she vaulted from the bed and raced across the hall.

"What is it?" she gasped.

"Can't you smell it?" he demanded, his eyes widened with outrage.

It didn't take Maggie any time at all to grasp the situation.

"Good heavens, Josh, you scared me to death."

He'd done the same thing to Ginny, it appeared, as her baby face crumpled into tears.

"There, there, Ginny, Daddy didn't mean to frighten you. He's just spoiled."

"What are you talking about? I'm not spoiled."

"Yes, you are. You expect everything to be easy." She reached for the treated wipes. "When she has a dirty diaper, you clean her with these."

"Okay," he hurriedly agreed, taking a step back. She handed him a wipe.

"You want me to…to change her?"

"That was the idea of you coming in here, wasn't it?"

"Yeah, but I didn't expect a dirty diaper. I can't—"

She stared at him, a challenge in her eyes.

"Come on, Maggie, you'll be better at it than—"

She shoved the wipe closer.

With a frown—and muttering something under his breath that she didn't ask him to repeat—Josh took the wipe. Undoing the tabs on the diaper, he carefully pulled it back, releasing the full force of the stench.

"Ugh! This is terrible."

Maggie said nothing, only reached over to pull another wipe out of the box. After glaring at her, Josh began the loathsome duty of cleanup. Five wipes later, including one to clean off her heel where Ginny had kicked in the wrong place, Josh had successfully completed the cleanup.

"Okay, I did it," he said, looking at Maggie.

"Good job. Now you'd better get a clean diaper on her before—"

Too late. Ginny liked being free of her diaper. It didn't seem to bother her that she wet all over herself.

"Babies are disgusting," Josh protested.

"They take after their daddies," Maggie suggested, grimacing in his direction. "I'll go rinse Ginny off in our bathroom and diaper and dress her. You wash your hands, strip the bed and clean it with disinfectant, put on a new sheet and go get the bottle."

Gathering a clean diaper, baby powder, fresh

clothes, a bath towel and Ginny, she left Josh staring at her and carried the baby to the master bath.

"I think your daddy has learned a lot this morning," she confided to the baby.

Ginny gurgled, happy to have more water to play in, and clapped her hands together.

By the time Josh appeared with the bottle, she and Ginny were cuddling in the bed. The bed with the pillow back in place.

Ginny reached out as soon as she saw the bottle. Maggie took advantage of that unusual occurrence. "Ginny wants you," she said, extending the baby toward her daddy.

"No, she doesn't. She just wants the bottle." He stuck the bottle out.

Ginny reached for it, but she couldn't quite touch it. When she puckered up, he put the nipple in her mouth. "She mustn't cry. Sam is still asleep."

"He slept through all that noise?" Maggie asked in surprise.

"Yeah, so feed Ginny before she cries again." He pulled the bottle out of the baby's mouth and tried to hand it to Maggie.

Ginny was becoming the object of a battle of wills. And Maggie was determined not to lose. She plopped Ginny down on Josh's side of the bed. "Josh, *you'd* better feed her."

Ginny had no idea what was going on, except that the bottle had been taken away. She climbed on the big pillow next to Maggie, her gaze glued to her objective, the bottle.

"Maggie, you're being difficult," Josh protested.

"No, I'm not. Even when you find someone to help you, you'll need to spend time with Ginny. You're her father."

Ginny whined, staring at the bottle.

"Yeah, but she'll cry if I pick her up!" Josh protested.

"Don't be silly. She wants her bottle. If you give it to her, she's not going to cry." She stared back at him, refusing to budge.

"Okay, I'll learn to deal with…whatever. But this weekend, with Sam here as my responsibility, it's not a good time to start. I mean, someone's trying to kill the guy."

Ginny let out a cry of protest at the lack of attention her needs were getting.

"She's going to start crying." Maggie's hands itched to grab the bottle and cuddle Ginny against her, but she knew she had to hold out—for both their sakes. Josh needed to come to terms with his baby.

He rounded the bed and sat down, propping the pillow behind him. Ginny, seeing the bottle close, lunged for it.

"Hey! You didn't tell me she could jump." He caught the baby and gave her the bottle. Ginny, half-sitting against him, lowered her mouth to the nipple.

"She can't get any milk that way, Josh. You have to hold her and keep the bottle raised."

He squared his back to the bed and picked Ginny up, dropping the bottle in the process. Ginny protested, her little baby hands stretching for it.

"Okay, okay, Gin, I'll get it," he said, grabbing the bottle with one hand while he held the little girl

with the other. Once the nipple returned to her mouth
and she began drinking, she had no interest in anything else.

"Kind of one-tracked, isn't she?" he asked, a half
grin on his lips that Maggie found enormously attractive. Of course, that attraction could also have something to do with the fact that Josh was only wearing
his pajama bottoms. Ginny certainly didn't have any
complaints about being held against his bare skin.

Maggie leaned back against her own pillow and
watched father and daughter.

"It's not as hard as I thought," Josh said, lifting
his gaze to her. "Though that earlier stuff was a pain.
How do people manage on their own?"

"They don't get everything cleaned up as fast. But
it's easier with two people." And much more enjoy-
able, she realized. Several times lately, she'd considered becoming a single parent. She still might. But
she was learning that when two people shouldered the
load, parenting was much sweeter.

And sexier.

Josh's solemn, sincere gaze, with those big blue
eyes so like his little girl's, was more than Maggie
could ignore. The time spent with these two was going to cost her. It would take her months to forget the
contentment of these days.

"Ginny and I appreciate what you're doing for us.
And I know I'm taking advantage of you, but I didn't
find a nanny yesterday and—"

"And you want me to help you Monday, too?"

"Is it too much to ask?"

"No. In fact, I think I need to take some vacation days. I've been working too much lately."

She couldn't bear the intimacy of the bed anymore. Not when she'd promised to stay longer. She didn't regret that promise, but she was going to have to be careful. She needed to harden her heart against Josh as much as possible. "I'll go start breakfast while you're taking care of Ginny."

Before she could escape, Josh had swung his legs over the side of the bed. "Ginny and I will come with you."

Three adults made his apartment seem small, Josh reflected. It had always been perfect for his life, until now. He'd never thought he would ever need to move.

But he was beginning to realize that Ginny was a permanent fixture in his life. And since he couldn't take time to care for her, he had to have room for a nanny or whoever.

With nothing else to do, he pulled the classifieds out of the paper and began reading the house-for-sale ads. "Hey, Maggie, listen to this. Four-bedroom house, three baths, large yard, Shawnee Mission School District."

She looked at him, surprised. Ginny had just awakened from her nap and was playing on the floor with Maggie, while Sam watched a golf tournament on television.

"Does that sound good?" he prompted when she said nothing.

"Good for what?"

"For Ginny."

"I thought you weren't going to move."

"I'll have to. There's not enough room here. And she'll need a yard to play in. And good schools to go to."

"It sounds expensive."

He dismissed her comment with a wave of his hand. "I've got some money saved."

He had quite a bit of money, actually, thanks to his mother. Her insistence that his father take a safe job, selling insurance, and insuring himself for an inordinate amount, had seemed silly. But when they'd had a car wreck while Josh was in college, killing both of his parents, he'd been left with a lot of money. He would rather have had parents.

He'd learned a valuable lesson, however. There was no protection against death.

"So, you're going to keep Ginny?"

He stared at Maggie. "What do you mean? Of course I'm going to keep Ginny! She's my child."

Sam was watching them, a strange expression on his face. "Isn't Maggie her mother?"

Josh ignored him, not willing to share his personal life with a client, but Maggie answered. "No, I'm not."

"I thought you were. The kid looks a lot like you." Sam turned his attention back to the television.

Josh stared at her in frustration. He wanted to discuss her meaning, to protest her thinking he would ever give up his child. But he didn't want to do that in front of Sam.

"Let's go into the bedroom," he suggested softly.

"Um, no, I have to fold clothes. I washed a load of Ginny's things." She got to her feet. "Watch Ginny for me."

The baby tried to crawl after Maggie, and Josh caught her around her little tummy. "Whoa, Ginny. Mommy—Maggie said for you to stay here."

His slip startled him. Maggie wasn't her mother, but she certainly acted like it. He knew she cared about Ginny. This morning, he'd thought he might win in their battle of wills over who was going to care for the baby, because he could see how hard it was for her to let him take her place.

But Maggie had surprised him.

And he'd surprised himself. It wasn't as hard to care for a baby as he'd thought. And she was kind of cute.

Ginny picked up a stuffed block and threw it.

He reached for the block and handed it back to her. In no time, she'd thrown it again. He handed it back. She threw it again.

"Wait a minute. This is a game, isn't it? I don't think I want to play," he said, then felt silly, arguing with a baby.

When Ginny reached for the block and squealed, he ignored her. Then she began crying.

"What's wrong with Ginny?" Maggie asked, a frown on her face as she rushed into the room, clean clothes filling her arms.

Josh immediately gave the block back to the baby.

"She's playing the throw-the-toy game," Sam muttered, his gaze fixed on the television.

Josh stared at him. He knew about Ginny's behavior? Oh, yeah, he'd said he had three kids. "She threw the block, and every time I brought it back to her, she threw it again. When I stopped, she cried," he said defensively. What was he supposed to have done?

"Why don't you take the ball and roll it to her. Then she can practice throwing it to you. Or close to you," Maggie added, a twinkle in her eyes.

Whatever made both females happy. Josh realized he didn't want either one of them upset with him. He played with Ginny for the next few minutes while Maggie folded baby clothes. It was a sweet, domestic scene—or would have been if Sam hadn't been there.

And if Josh had the right to cuddle Maggie.

Distracted, he hadn't noticed Ginny crawling to his side. When he felt a tug on his shirt, he discovered his baby standing beside him. "Maggie, look! She can stand."

"I know. Careful, Ginny, or you'll fall." The baby beamed at Maggie, then at Josh. "It won't be long before she can walk," Maggie added. "At least I think so. Nathan has been taking a few steps."

"Who's Nathan?" Sam asked.

"My nephew, who's just over a year old."

"Girls learn faster than boys," Sam said, still staring at the television.

"They do?" Josh was surprised that his house guest knew so much.

"Yeah, my son didn't walk until he was almost eighteen months, but the girls were walking by the time they turned one."

"You have two girls and a boy?" Maggie asked politely.

"Yep. They really keep you hopping." He turned to Josh. "You don't get much peace with little ones around."

"I can imagine," Josh agreed as he grabbed Ginny. She'd lost her balance and was taking a nosedive. Unperturbed by her near accident, she grabbed Josh's nose and grinned at him.

"Oh, dear, I forgot to call Susan. May I use the phone?" Maggie asked.

"Sure. How's she doing?"

"Fine. Still determined to make it without any help," Maggie admitted with a sigh. "But we love her. I usually do something with her and the kids on the weekend, so I need to let her know I can't this weekend."

"If it will cause problems, I can—" Josh began reluctantly.

"No. She'll understand. She always does." Maggie's smile said a lot about her relationship with her new sister.

He returned to his playing with Ginny, listening to the one-sided conversation. When Maggie hung up, he was able to turn his attention back to their situation.

"We've got to come up with a good plan to get you to the trial on Monday," he said to Sam. "Just in case they decide to make another try."

Both Sam and Maggie stiffened, looking anxious.

Someone knocked on the door.

Chapter Seven

Josh felt sure Pete, who was on duty this afternoon, would have alerted him to problems, but he motioned for silence anyway. It didn't pay to take chances.

Through the peephole, he saw a man in a green uniform. Turning, he motioned to Maggie. "Is this a guy from the diner?" he whispered.

She peeped through the hole and then nodded. "Yes, it's Joey, the deliveryman." Without asking for permission, she opened the door. "Hi, Joey. Come on in."

"Thanks, Maggie. Much longer and the food would be cold." He was short and a little on the plump side, like Sam.

"What are we eating this afternoon?" Maggie asked.

"Chicken and dumplings. And Kate sent a message. She said she was coming with me in the morning to deliver breakfast."

"She can't do that," Maggie protested. "She has her family to look after."

Joey grinned. "And she said to tell you no fussing."

"Why is your sister coming?" Josh demanded.

Maggie and Joey exchanged a smile before she answered him. "Kate's worried. She's afraid you're taking advantage of me."

"You won't let her talk you into leaving, will you?" asked Josh. He frowned, wrinkling the bandage on his forehead.

"Of course not." Once Kate saw Ginny, Maggie knew she'd believe Maggie was doing the right thing.

Joey soon packed up and left. After the door closed behind him, Sam asked, "I thought you and Maggie were married?"

"We are," Josh said hurriedly, shooting Maggie a warning look.

"Oh. Then why would her sister talk her into leaving?"

Josh couldn't seem to come up with an answer, and Maggie helped him out. "She's upset because I'm taking off work instead of Josh to care for Ginny."

"Ah. My wife and I had several arguments about that, but I was making the most money." He turned his attention back to the food. "They sure do make good food."

"Yeah," Josh agreed, but he had a thoughtful look on his face.

After eating for several minutes in silence, Josh repeated his earlier warning. "I hate to be the bearer of bad tidings, but the word is out that your enemies intend to ice you Monday morning. We've got to figure out a good way to get you to the trial."

Maggie caught her breath. Josh had already been shot once because he was with Sam. That meant Monday morning he would be in danger again.

"Josh, if anything should happen to you, who will— I mean, have you provided for Ginny? Who will take her?"

He appeared irritated by her question, but it was important, in Maggie's mind. Not that she wanted to think about anything happening to Josh, but Ginny had already lost one parent.

"Not now, Maggie. I have to think about how to disguise Sam."

"He could dress as a woman. That's how they always manage it on television," Maggie suggested, eager to solve this problem so they could move on to the more important one.

"Yeah, television. That takes a master actor. Any acting experience, Sam?"

Sam shook his head, panic on his face. "I should have never stuck my nose in where it didn't belong. I don't want to be a witness."

"Come on, Sam, you'll be breaking up an illegal operation that's hurt a lot of people."

Sam looked unconvinced. "That won't comfort my kids any, or my wife, if I don't make it back home."

Suddenly, Maggie had the answer. "I know how you can do it."

Josh frowned at her, as if he found her words intrusive. "Maggie, you'd best leave this to the professional here, me."

"You don't want my idea?"

"Maggie—"

"He switches places with Joey."

She watched as her words penetrated Josh's mind. With a dawning smile, he nodded. "You know, I think that's brilliant."

"So you owe me an apology," she said, smiling in return.

He stood and pulled her to her feet. Before Maggie knew what he intended, he kissed her. A big, congratulatory smack, followed by an even bigger smile.

"I do," he assured her. His arms dropped to her waist and he leaned toward her again. Maggie caught her breath, sure he intended to repeat that kiss. Only with less smack and more—

"I don't get it," Sam interrupted.

Maggie's heart dipped as Josh released her and faced Sam again, distracted from his intent.

"Think, Sam. If those men have been watching the apartment, they've seen Joey delivering food, twice already, and he's coming tomorrow morning. He wears a distinctive green coverall, and he's about your size."

"We don't look that much alike," Sam said nervously.

"Without your glasses you do," Maggie said.

"I can't see a thing without my glasses."

"We'll fix that," Josh said dismissively. "People see what they expect to see. By Monday morning, they won't even give Joey a close look. It's perfect." Josh turned back to Maggie. "Thanks, sweetheart."

"But I can't see without my glasses," Sam repeated, upset.

"Do you have prescription sunglasses with you?" Josh asked.

"Yes, of course, but—"

"Maggie, can we get Joey to start wearing sunglasses that look similar to Sam's, starting in the morning?"

"Yes, of course, I'll call the diner."

"Wait, we need to go over all the details. The van, is it an automatic?"

"I can't drive a stick shift," Sam protested.

Maggie was growing irritated with the man's attitude. They were trying to help him. "The van is a stick shift."

"Hmmm," Josh said, rubbing his chin. "If I go with him, it will look suspicious."

"Kate! Kate's coming tomorrow. If she drives tomorrow and then comes on Monday, too, she can— but I can't put Kate in danger."

"There shouldn't be much danger, but we can't ask your sister to participate unless she agrees to the risk. Do you think she will?"

Knowing Kate's daring nature, Maggie suspected she'd enjoy such a thing. But Will might never speak to Maggie again.

"I think I'd better call Kate and talk to her."

An hour later everything was settled. Will had, as Maggie predicted, objected to Kate's participation. However, much to Maggie's surprise, he had suggested that he himself accompany Joey the next day

and on Monday morning. He would drive and escort
Sam to the courtroom.

Kate had promised to find sunglasses for Joey that
resembled the ones Sam wore. Plans were made for
Joey after Sam left, so he wouldn't be in any danger.

"You're going to have to leave the apartment, too,
sweetheart," Josh said, a frown on his face.

Maggie didn't think he even realized he'd ad-
dressed her with the endearment, but she enjoyed it
anyway. "Why?"

"Because they'll come inside to check after a
while. I want you and Ginny out of here." He was
going over a list he'd made. Maggie was discovering
how thorough he was.

"Can you go to the diner? Or I'll pay for a hotel
room for the day."

"We can go back to my apartment."

"That's too far away. And you'd be alone. I want
someone around, just in case."

"What about Sam's family?" she suddenly asked
in a whisper. Sam again was watching television
while they were in the kitchen. "What if they go after
his family?"

"We sent them out of town yesterday afternoon."

Yes, he was definitely thorough.

"Josh, we need to talk about Ginny."

"Is something wrong with her?" he asked, sudden
tension on his face.

Maggie reveled in the concern she saw there. He
loved his baby girl, even if he didn't realize it yet.
"No, she's fine. She's playing in the playpen. But
you need to think about providing for her. You have

to designate someone as guardian for her in case—in case something happens.''

His frown deepened. "You're right. I hadn't thought of that. But accidents can happen to anyone, not just private investigators.''

Maggie wasn't sure what he was trying to say. "I know that. But—''

"I'm not going to stop being a P.I.''

She shook her head in bewilderment. "Of course not.''

"Of course not?" He leaned forward. "You're not telling me I need to change my job?''

"No. You'll have to find someone to take care of Ginny with your odd hours. It doesn't matter when you see Ginny, as long as you spend time with her. But—''

"Do you really mean that?''

Maggie felt as if she were wading through mud. It took a lot of energy with little to show for the effort. "Josh, I don't understand what you're getting at.''

"I know you don't," he agreed, and surprised her with a warm smile. "But that's okay.''

"What I'm trying to say is you need to provide for Ginny.''

"Okay. Let me get a piece of paper.''

He left the kitchen, and Maggie sat at the table, still confused. He thought she would try to make him give up his job?

Almost at once he returned to the kitchen. "If something happens to me, will you take care of Ginny? I already know you love her.''

Warmth flooded through Maggie. Warm gratitude

that he would trust her. Warm love for the wriggly little girl in the other room. Warm hope for the future. "Of course I will. But...but don't you have family?"

"No. Well, yes, a distant cousin in Boston, but I don't know her. I want Ginny to have someone who loves her. There'll be plenty of money, so you won't have to work, and—"

"Are you saying I have to give up *my* job for Ginny?"

"She'll need someone to take care of her."

"So you're giving up your job?"

"You just said you wouldn't ask that of me!" he exclaimed, taking a step away from the table.

"But you have no difficulty asking that of me?"

"But you're a—"

"Woman?" She waited patiently for the parallel to hit him.

Enlightenment didn't strike him at once.

"But women are supposed to—there's sufficient money—"

"So you don't need to work, either?" She sat, waiting, watching as color filled his cheeks.

"Maggie, you don't understand," he protested.

She said nothing.

Finally, he sat down at the table. "Maybe I'm the one who doesn't understand. I didn't mean you had to quit your job if something happens to me. I know you'd do what's right for Ginny."

Maggie smiled. "Thank you, Josh, for trusting me."

Josh's earlier conversation with Maggie left him stunned. He had been asking almost the same sacrifice of her that his mother had asked of his father.

Her patience with him had amazed him, too. She hadn't lost her temper or accused him of trying to ruin her life. She'd simply said she would care for Ginny.

And he had no doubt of that.

"Josh, it's time for Ginny to go to bed," Maggie said from the doorway.

"Okay. Want me to kiss her good-night?"

Maggie smiled. "I hope you do, of course. I laid out her nightgown and a clean diaper for you."

Ginny babbled something from the playpen, but Maggie didn't respond to the baby, and she also didn't cross the room to pick her up.

His mind on everything that had gone on tonight, it took Josh a minute to realize Maggie wasn't going to put the baby to bed. "Maggie?"

"Yes, Josh?" she answered from the doorway.

"Look, I know I'm her father, but—"

"But?"

"Can't you put her to bed? She'll be happier."

Sam, watching television as usual, said without turning his head, "My daughters love for me to tuck them in."

Josh rolled his eyes. "She's a baby."

"Got to start sometime," Sam muttered.

It was easy for Sam to say. He didn't have to do anything. Josh got up and looked at Maggie. "Will you help me?"

"Of course," Maggie assured him with a smile that lit up her face.

He held out his arms to his baby daughter. Much to his delighted surprise, she chuckled and reached for him.

Cradling her against him, he walked to the doorway. "I'm a little suspicious. You don't think she has another surprise for me, do you?"

"No, I don't. But you dealt with it once. You can do it again," Maggie assured him.

And to win her approval he would even take on that chore again. Hey, he thought, when had Maggie's approval become so important to him?

He discovered preparing for bedtime could be sweetly pleasant. Ginny was a happy baby, smiling even as she rubbed her eyes. When he'd gotten those lively arms and legs snapped into some pajamas covered with kittens, he cuddled her against him, dropping a kiss on her forehead.

Maggie leaned toward him to kiss Ginny, too, and Josh found himself abruptly distracted from the baby. He wanted Maggie to lean into him for other purposes.

"You're doing a fine job of tending to Ginny," she said after she'd kissed the baby.

"It's not too hard with you here to give me confidence," he assured her. He put Ginny in her bed, covering her with a blanket and winding the mobile. As the baby watched the dangling animals, they turned off the overhead light, leaving only the nightlight to illuminate the mobile, and slipped from the room.

"Now what?" he asked as they paused in the hall.

"I don't know. I think I'm getting cabin fever," Maggie confessed.

"Cabin fever?"

"I haven't been outside the apartment in several days."

Somehow the thought of Maggie leaving, even if she promised to return, disturbed him. "How about we watch a movie or play a game?"

"What kind of game?"

"I have the original Trivial Pursuit, or we could play cards. I'm sure Sam would like a new diversion, too."

Soon the three of them were seated in the kitchen, popcorn on the table, testing each other with trivia questions. Josh found himself fascinated with Maggie, watching her responses.

He even grew jealous as Sam exhibited a dry wit that tickled Maggie. Her cheeks flushed, her hazel eyes flashed, and he wanted her attention centered only on him. When their hands met in the popcorn bowl, he felt a stirring deep in his loins.

"Don't you know the answer?" Maggie asked.

Josh had no idea what the question had been. He asked Sam to repeat it.

"What quarterback served in the Navy before leading his team to several Super Bowls?" Sam read.

"I think I need a clue," Josh said, leaning toward Maggie.

"A clue? Don't you watch football?" Maggie asked.

"Yeah. Do *you?*"

"Of course. Though I mostly watch the Chiefs."

Had he died and gone to heaven? A woman as sweet as Maggie who watched football? With his gaze focused on her lips, he leaned closer still.

"Do you know the answer or don't you?" Sam demanded.

"Yeah. Roger Staubach," he tossed off, his gaze never leaving Maggie.

"You were teasing me. You knew the answer all along," Maggie protested.

Before he could respond—or kiss her, as he wanted to do—Sam was urging him to roll the dice. Josh was about ready to give Sam up to his enemies. He wanted to have Maggie all to himself.

An hour later the game ended when Maggie had won all her pieces of the plastic pie. Josh was glad they had finished. It was time to retire to the bedroom. And the bed. He was looking forward to holding Maggie in his arms.

If he could contain himself.

"Is something wrong?" Maggie asked.

He smoothed the frown away. "No, of course not. Ready for bed? We'll be up early with Ginny in the morning."

Now she was the one looking worried. "Um, yes. I'll just put these glasses in the dishwasher."

He fetched the bedding for the couch and told Sam good-night as Maggie came out of the kitchen.

She acted nervous as she, too, said good-night to Sam. Then she hurried down the hall, not waiting for Josh.

"Are you that sleepy?" he asked as he entered the bedroom behind her.

"No. Not at all. Um, do you want the bathroom first?"

"You go ahead. I'll wait."

He listened to the shower, imagining her naked under the spray of water, and decided his own shower would have to be a cold one. When everything was settled Monday, he and Maggie were going to have to have a long talk. He didn't intend to let her go.

She came out, buttoned to her chin in that white cotton robe. "Your turn."

Maggie let out a deep sigh when the bathroom door closed behind Josh. She wished she could crawl into bed and pretend to be asleep when he came out. But she couldn't.

Because she couldn't sleep in the bed with him.

Last night, each time she woke up, she'd found herself in Josh's arms. Returning to the same bed with the man would only lead to disaster. Even if he didn't want their…closeness to lead to anything else, she couldn't trust herself, lulled by sleep, to keep her distance. His sexiness tempted her. His big heart tempted her even more.

How she longed to be a family with Ginny and Josh. It couldn't happen, of course. But she knew that the major reason she'd so willingly come with Josh had been her yearning for more.

After her father died, she realized she'd been hiding from life. And his death made it clear to her that time was precious. Her father hadn't talked to Susan, hadn't told her he was her father, before he died. He'd intended to, but he hadn't had time.

Maggie had been hiding from life because she was afraid of failing. She trusted only numbers, not people. Then Kate had married Will and had baby Nathan, and Maggie had seen her sister transformed by a happiness Kate had never known before.

Maggie wasn't jealous. Not exactly. But her sister's situation had started her thinking about changing her own life. Finding happiness while she still had time.

And it was just about then that Josh McKinley, with baby Ginny, had walked into the diner.

"You're not in bed yet?" Josh asked.

Maggie jumped. Lost in her thoughts, she hadn't heard him emerge from the bathroom. "N-no. I need to check on Ginny." She hurried from the room.

She stood in the semidark, staring at the beautiful baby who had come to mean so much to her in such a short time. Finally, hoping Josh had gone to sleep, she slipped back into his bedroom. It was dark, but the hall light showed her the outline of his body on the far side of the bed.

"Is she all right?" he called softly.

"Yes. Fine."

"Come to bed, Maggie. It's late and you must be tired."

She swallowed, shifting from one foot to the other, unsure what to do. "Um, in a minute." She dashed to the bathroom door.

When she emerged from the bath five minutes later, having sat on the edge of the tub, waiting, hoping Josh would go to sleep, he remained silent.

She tiptoed across the room. The large king-size pillows that she'd used to separate the bed area last night were on the floor. Trying to avoid making noise, she placed the two pillows, end to end, on the floor by her side of the bed. Then she pulled a blanket from the top of the closet.

Having made herself a reasonably comfortable nest that would preclude the warmth of Josh's arms, she settled down with a sigh. And with longing.

Josh kept his breathing even, unmoving, waiting for her to get in the bed. He knew he couldn't pull her into his arms while she was awake.

She would protest.

But she was a sound sleeper. And a natural cuddler. He loved holding her against him.

He opened his eyes when her breathing became even, but she had yet to get in the bed. Slowly he raised himself up and searched for her. She wasn't in sight.

Slipping out of the bed, he rounded it to check in Ginny's room and almost tripped over Maggie, asleep on the floor.

He shook his head, a tender smile filling him. Without hesitation, he scooped her up into his arms, placed her on the bed, then went to his side.

He slid under the covers, pulling them over her, also. Then, as he had the night before, he slid his arms around her, holding her against him. Contentment filled him, and he closed his eyes.

Chapter Eight

Josh had paid for his contentment.

It was Monday morning, time to concentrate on getting Sam to court safely, and Josh had trouble thinking of anything but Maggie's anger. She would scarcely speak to him.

And last night she'd slept on the floor in Ginny's room.

He dressed for the demands of the day and hurried to the living room. Will and Joey were due any minute with breakfast, and they wouldn't have much time to eat before Sam and Will left.

Pasting a smile on his face, hoping Maggie was in a more amenable mood this morning, he stepped into the living room only to find Maggie sitting in his favorite chair, her arms crossed, tears running down her face.

"Maggie? Maggie, what's wrong?"

She glowered at him but didn't answer.

He crossed the room and fell to his knees in front of her, taking her hands in his. "Are you all right?"

"I'm fine. I'm so mad I could spit, but I'm fine."

"Maggie, I didn't bother you last night. Why are you still mad at me?" Had it been such a terrible sin to hold her?

"Not you! I—"

A knock on the door interrupted them. Josh, his mind still on Maggie, automatically moved to the door and checked through the peephole. Seeing Will and Joey, he opened the door, letting them in. Before they'd even crossed the threshold, he turned back to Maggie.

"What's wrong, sweetheart? Did Sam do something?"

"No. Never mind. You don't have time."

"Is Ginny all right?"

"Yes. Go eat some breakfast."

She was right. There was no time for a heart-to-heart, but he wished there were. "Okay, you come eat, too. Have you got you and Ginny packed up for the day? You can't stay here, you know."

"I know. I'm going to take Ginny to Will and Kate's. The doctor said Nate isn't contagious anymore."

"All right. I'll pick you up there, once I get Sam squared away. You're not to come back here alone. You understand?" He wasn't taking any chances on Maggie and Ginny getting hurt.

"Of course I understand. I'm not an idiot!"

Whoops. Looks like he'd tromped on a sore spot. "I know you're not an idiot. You're brilliant. You're

the one who came up with our escape plan." He
risked her anger by kissing her briefly, but it was
worth the risk. He'd been dying to kiss her sweet
mouth for the past twenty-four hours.

"Hey, you two, break it up and come eat," Will
said from the kitchen doorway.

Maggie's cheeks flamed and Josh wanted to warm
his hands against her hot skin. Instead, he pulled her
from the chair, keeping her hand in his as they headed
to the kitchen. Whatever had upset her earlier had
transferred her anger from him to someone else. He
could only be grateful.

Sam had joined Will and Joey in the kitchen. He
was eating, but he looked pale and nervous.

"Maggie, you and Ginny are going to our house,
aren't you?" Will asked.

"Yes. We'll slip out right after you and Sam. And
you'll call as soon as you can?"

"Sure. Kate would kill me if I didn't," Will assured her with a grin. Then he turned to Josh. "It's
a good thing you're not married. These women like
to keep track of a guy."

A quick look at Sam showed Josh he was too concerned with the coming events to notice that Will had
disclosed that Josh and Maggie were not husband and
wife after all.

"You don't seem to be suffering," Josh pointed
out. He hadn't met Will until yesterday, but he liked
the man. Was even impressed with him. The guy ran
a multimillion-dollar company, but he seemed down-
to-earth.

Will's face softened, a greater testament to his

happy marriage than any words he could speak. "No, I'm not suffering. Life couldn't be better, in fact."

"Shouldn't we be leaving?" Sam asked, his voice shaking.

Will looked at Josh, raising an eyebrow in question.

"Yeah. Probably so. You'll have a little extra time, Will, so take a circuitous route, as if you had some more deliveries to make. You remember the instructions for when you get to the courthouse?"

"Yeah. We'll be fine. I'll see you there." Will stood, then turned to Maggie. "You get yourself and Ginny safely over to Kate's, okay?"

"I will," Maggie agreed solemnly.

"They'll be fine. There's no danger, as long as they aren't here." Josh had to believe what he'd said, because the thought of Maggie and Ginny in danger wasn't something he could handle. He escorted Will and Sam to the door. Once he closed it behind them, Joey and Maggie joined him at the window, trying to see their exit. Both men were wearing the bright green coveralls of the Lucky Charm.

When the van pulled away from the curb without interference or signs of anyone following them, Josh let out the breath he'd been holding.

"Okay. Joey, open the door and call Pete in. Time for phase two."

When Joey stepped out into the hall, Josh turned around and clasped Maggie's upper arms. Her startled look told him she hadn't anticipated his touching her.

"You take care of yourself and Ginny." Then he covered her beautiful lips with his, wishing he could accompany her to Kate's house, just to be sure she and the baby were safe. But he couldn't.

Someone cleared his throat behind them, and Josh reluctantly let Maggie go. "We'll talk this afternoon, okay?"

Her eyes widened and she nodded but said nothing.

"Go get Ginny."

When she reappeared only seconds later with his daughter snuggled against her, he drew a deep breath. "You got everything?"

She nodded again, pointing to the diaper bag she had slung over her shoulder. "If I don't, Kate will have what I need."

He drew another deep breath. What was wrong with him? He'd never had such difficulty parting from anyone. Ignoring the two men watching them, he stepped to Maggie's side and wrapped both females in his arms.

To his delight, Maggie didn't resist. Instead, she raised her free hand and stroked his cheek. "Take care," she whispered and kissed him gently, then stepped out of his arms and walked toward the door.

"Maggie," he called, then stopped.

She turned to look at him, Ginny babbling nonsense in her arms. "Yes?"

"You, too," he muttered, unable to say what had first flashed into his mind. He didn't love her. He didn't ever intend to love anyone. It would give that person too much power.

But he cared about her...and Ginny.

Yes, that was it. He cared about her.

"I will," she assured him and walked out the door.

The three men turned back to the window. It would take longer for Maggie to appear on the street because she was walking to the parking garage.

There was no danger, Josh assured himself. The bad guys didn't even know about Maggie and Ginny. They would think she was coming from one of the other condos.

But a heavy sigh escaped him when he saw Maggie's compact pull out into the street and drive away.

"Okay, guys, time for phase three," he muttered.

When Kate opened the door for Maggie, who had Ginny propped on one hip, she embraced both of them.

"You're all right!" Kate exclaimed as she backed up to let them enter.

"Of course we are. We were never in danger. Have you heard from Will?"

"Not yet. He said not to expect a call until after ten, when the trial is to start again, and it's only a couple of minutes after nine." Kate led Maggie toward the kitchen.

"Ginny's a darling baby, Maggie, but this whole situation is a problem," Kate said firmly as she gestured for her sister to sit at the kitchen table.

Maggie greeted Betty, Kate's housekeeper and almost a family member. "How are you?"

"Fine. And glad to see you safe and sound. Coffee?"

"That would be great." Then Maggie turned to deal with her sister's remark. "She is a darling, isn't she?"

"You're going to ignore the rest?" Kate demanded, raising one brow.

"Yes. Where's Nathan?"

"He's upstairs playing. Angie is with him. Want to take Ginny upstairs? And then we'll talk."

Maggie knew there was no escape. When Kate was determined, nothing stood in her way. Maggie followed Kate's plan, delivering Ginny to Angie, the nanny who took care of Nathan while Kate was at the diner.

When they were once more seated around the kitchen table, their coffee supplemented by warm cinnamon rolls, Kate didn't waste a minute.

"When are you going to go back home?"

"I promised Josh I would stay today."

"Has he found someone to take care of Ginny?"

"No, he hasn't had a chance to, what with the witness thing." She looked up from her coffee cup. "I apologize for getting you and Will involved."

Kate waved away her concern. "I think Will has really enjoyed it. And I don't think he's in any danger."

"I hope not. But Josh was shot when he escorted Sam into town and—" She broke off, regretting her words as she saw a flare of alarm in Kate's eyes. "I shouldn't have said that. I know the plan is a good one."

"Yes, it is. And Josh does have a solid reputation. Will checked."

Maggie raised one eyebrow.

"Well, I wasn't going to let you go off with some man that I knew nothing about!" Kate stretched out a hand toward Maggie. "We may have added a sister, but our family is still small."

"So if you had a big family, you'd let me go off with any old man," Maggie teased, knowing the answer before Kate protested.

"No, of course not, but…Maggie, you're not very experienced."

Maggie couldn't meet her sister's concerned look. Not that she'd done anything she should be ashamed of, but maybe, just maybe, she'd wanted to.

"He hasn't hurt you, has he?" Kate asked in response to Maggie's behavior.

"No, of course not."

"So tomorrow everything will be normal again."

Maggie pressed her lips together. Finally, she said, "Not exactly."

"What's happened?" Kate asked, her tone ominous, as if Maggie were only fulfilling a prediction her sister had already made.

"I quit my job."

"What?" Kate squeaked. Even Betty turned away from the sink where she was cleaning to stare at Maggie.

Maggie understood their shock. She'd clung to her job at the accounting firm through everything, always talking about how important her career was. She'd worked hard to move up the corporate ladder, and she'd put in long hours.

"What happened?" Kate asked.

"I called this morning to take a week's vacation. I told my boss I had a family emergency. He told me I had to come to work." She kept her gaze on her clasped hands, wondering if Kate would think she'd behaved foolishly. Finally, she looked at her sister. "I snapped. I'd given so much time to my work. Now that I needed some time away, they couldn't be generous."

"Good for you," Kate said, reaching over to cover Maggie's hands. "I told you they took advantage of you."

"Good for me? I'm without a job, Kate. How am I going to support myself?"

She shouldn't have asked that question. She knew how Kate would react.

"Will will give you a job. He always needs good accountants."

"Poor Will. He didn't know when he married you that he'd have to employ your entire family," Maggie said with a wry chuckle.

"The only family member he offered a job to was Susan. You know she refused."

"Yes," Maggie agreed with a sigh. And she understood why Susan had refused. Their newest sister had a lot of pride, and the job Will had offered her paid too well. Susan thought she was being given charity.

"But you won't refuse, will you?"

"Yes, I will. It's bad enough that I'm working for you. I don't need to be working for Will, too."

"But what are you going to do?"

Though she'd protested Kate's approval of her quitting, Maggie had already formed a plan in her head. "Well, the Lucky Charm is doing so well, I might even be able to scrape by on what you pay me to do the books and my share of the profit. I thought I might try to pick up a few more clients. Sort of start my own business.''

Kate responded at once. ''That's a terrific idea! You'll be rich in no time. Maggie, I'm so proud of you!''

''I haven't done it yet,'' she warned, then she admitted, ''but I've been wanting to make some changes in my life.'' She thought of the baby upstairs and the man who was in danger, and she knew some changes had already occurred.

She only hoped those changes wouldn't break her heart.

Josh pulled into the long, elegant driveway that led to Kate and Will's beautiful home, a sigh easing its way through his tired body.

Sam had given his testimony and was feeling quite proud of himself. Don and Pete were going to escort him home in the morning after spending the night in a hotel. Will had done his part safely and had returned home.

Now it was time for Josh to collect Ginny and, he hoped, Maggie. He'd just asked for her to stay until today, but he didn't want her to leave. Because he cared about her.

And because he liked having her in his life.

Just because of Ginny, he assured himself. After all, he knew better than to get involved with a woman. But his daughter needed Maggie.

Parking, he got out of his car and knocked on the door. He was surprised when Maggie was the one who answered. Unprepared to see her at once, he went with his instincts and swept her up into his arms, hugging her tightly against him.

"Are you and Ginny okay?" he whispered, his face buried in her hair.

"We're fine. How about you?" She pulled her head back to examine him. "No one shot at you?"

"Nope. The shooting the other day was rare, Maggie. It's the first time I've ever been wounded on the job, I promise." He didn't want her thinking he was some gunslinger, endangering himself at every turn.

She ran a finger over the scar still visible from the glancing blow he'd sustained Friday.

He let her slide down his body until her feet reached the floor. But he didn't let her go. A man needed a little comfort, a little reward, after a hard day.

And that was the only reason he kissed her, of course.

"Come on in," Kate called from somewhere behind Maggie.

Josh reluctantly lifted his lips from Maggie's and eyed her sister. He hadn't actually spoken to her before, but he had the idea that she wasn't happy with him.

"Uh, hello, you must be Kate."

"Yes, I'm Kate. Maggie's sister."

He glanced at Maggie, a half smile on his lips. She shrugged her shoulders at him, as if saying she couldn't stop her sister from asking him questions.

"I'm glad to meet you. Will was certainly a help

this morning. He's talked to you, hasn't he? You know he's safe?''

"Yes, he called a little after ten. Would you care for a cup of coffee, Josh?''

"I thought Maggie and Ginny might be ready to go home.'' He knew *he* was. He wanted to be alone with Maggie. After all, he had to find out what had caused her to cry this morning.

"You can spare the time for Josh to have a cup of coffee, can't you, Maggie?'' Kate asked insistently.

Maggie smiled at Josh. "You may as well accept it, Josh. Kate is going to cross-examine you.''

Her smile made even that prospect acceptable. "I have nothing to hide.''

Kate lifted one eyebrow, as if she didn't believe him, then turned and led the way into the kitchen. "I hope you don't mind being informal. We all prefer the kitchen.'' She and Maggie sat down.

"Me, too. Where's Ginny?'' he asked Maggie as he seated himself.

"She's asleep upstairs,'' she replied. "Kate's nanny, Angie, has helped take care of her today. She's been very happy.''

"Good. Is Angie looking for a job? I could hire her away from Kate,'' Josh said, grinning at Kate to let her know he was teasing.

"No, she's not looking for a job. But I can give you the name of the agency who sent her to us,'' Kate said. "After all, you can't count on Maggie as a permanent solution.''

Her words were only what Josh had told himself,

but he didn't like hearing them. "Of course not. Maggie's been more than generous with her time."

"So, when are you going to hire someone to take care of Ginny?" Kate pressed.

"As soon as we get back to the apartment, I'll start making calls," he promised, trying to hide his resentment that Kate was pushing Maggie away from him.

"Kate, this is none of your business," Maggie warned.

Josh started to speak, to assure Maggie that he understood Kate's concern, when Kate spoke first.

"Maggie, you don't even have a job anymore because of this man and—"

"What? What happened to your job?" Josh demanded. "Was that why you were crying this morning? What did those people do?" He was half out of his chair, ready to slug someone for being mean to Maggie, before he even realized it.

She tugged on his arm. "Sit down. Everything's fine. I've decided it was for the best."

"What happened?" he repeated, his jaw clenched.

"My boss told me I couldn't have any vacation days this week, and...and I quit."

He stared at Maggie, turned to look at Kate for confirmation, and faced Maggie again. "You quit your job for Ginny?"

"No. I quit for myself. I haven't been happy with my job for some time, Josh. You and Ginny were the catalyst, but I did what I wanted to do. It was my decision, and you're not to blame."

"But what are you going to do? Will you look for another accounting job?"

She explained about her idea to build a small firm, doing books for small companies.

"Hey, I could use your services."

"I don't need charity. I've already told Kate that. I'll be just fine," Maggie assured him.

"Of course you will," he agreed. "But I'm serious. I've recently started thinking about hiring someone. The paperwork is taking up too much of my time."

"Josh—we'll talk about it later," Maggie said, shaking her head no.

But her words were an encouragement to Josh. He was pleased that she at least intended to talk to him after today. He didn't want to lose contact with her.

"So," Maggie continued, "I'm free to care for Ginny for a couple of more days if you need me."

"Maggie!" Kate protested.

"Of course I need you," Josh said at the same time. Then he and Kate glared at each other.

Will's entrance into the kitchen eased the tension a little. "Greetings. How's everyone doing? The rest of the day go all right, Josh?"

Josh said hello and assured Will that their adventure had ended well.

"If that's true, then why are you and Kate shooting daggers at each other?" Will asked.

Kate didn't wait for anyone else to answer her husband. "Because he's still taking advantage of Maggie."

"I'm not taking advantage of her. She offered."

"Maggie spends too much time taking care of

everyone else," Kate protested. "Someone should be taking care of her!"

"I'm willing to take care of Maggie!" Josh returned, continuing to do battle with Kate.

"Please! I'm not an incompetent doofus!" Maggie said, rising to her feet. "If I choose to spend some days with Ginny, to give Josh time to find appropriate care, that's my business, Kate."

Her sister looked somewhat contrite, though not completely convinced. "He's never going to find anyone to give Ginny twenty-four-hour care, unless he marries someone."

"I know, but—"

Kate's words reminded Josh of the idea he'd had earlier. He didn't wait to consider his impulse. It felt too right. He cleared his throat and took the plunge. "So, will you marry me, Maggie?"

Chapter Nine

"**Y**ou're in love with Maggie?" Kate demanded, a beaming smile on her face.

"No!" Josh retorted, leaping to his feet. "No, I'm not. I'm offering her a marriage of convenience. I'll take care of her, and she'll take care of Ginny."

His answer didn't please Kate. "How dare you! How insulting to my sister. She doesn't have to settle for that kind of marriage!" Little did Josh know that Kate had almost "settled" for that kind of marriage herself—but happily she and Will had become enamoured of each other and ended with a love match.

"Honey, you're not the one he's asking," Will said quietly. But he frowned at Josh.

Josh looked at Maggie, fear filling him. Would she react the same way? Would she walk away from him, not even giving him the couple of days she'd promised? "Maggie—"

"How soon do I have to answer?"

Her quiet question brought a response from all three adults.

"Maggie, don't be too hasty," Will warned.

"Mary Margaret O'Connor, don't you dare accept that lukewarm offer!" Kate insisted.

"Take all the time you need, sweetheart," Josh said softly, hope filling his heart. "But it would work. You'd have a place to live while you started your business. You could stay home with Ginny while you worked. And…and we've done pretty well the past few days."

"Maggie!" Kate protested again.

Maggie stood. "I think we should go now. I'll call you tomorrow, Kate."

Josh rose, too, but Will stopped him. "Have you checked your condo since this morning?"

"No, I was too anxious to get to Maggie and Ginny." He couldn't believe he hadn't thought of that necessity. What kind of private investigator was he? "Maggie, would you stay here while I go see if it's inhabitable?"

"Yes, but you shouldn't go alone. I'll leave Ginny here for a few minutes and go with you."

He really didn't think there was any danger, so he held out his hand to her in acceptance.

"No!" both Kate and Will exclaimed. Then Will added, "I'll go with you, Josh. Just in case there's a problem."

Josh would've preferred Maggie's company, though he had nothing against Will. But the man was right. He shouldn't take any risks with Maggie.

With a brief nod in her direction, Josh headed for

the front door. The sooner he checked out the condo,
the sooner he'd be alone with Maggie.

The moment they were alone, Kate started lecturing
Maggie on the drawbacks of even considering Josh's
proposal. Maggie listened without speaking for at
least ten minutes before she put a halt to Kate's
words.

"Kate, I'm a full-grown woman. And I want a fam-
ily, a chance at happiness, like you. I…I care about
Josh. He may not love me, but he needs me. And
Ginny is so special."

"Honey, you can have your own baby."

"Yes, and maybe I will someday, but that's no reason not to love Ginny. I have to think about everything. So, let's change the subject now and talk about
something more interesting."

Fortunately Kate knew when to quit. She began
discussing Nathan's latest accomplishments, comparing her little genius with Ginny, predicting what
Ginny would be doing soon, also.

As an interesting topic, it almost topped Maggie's
list. Almost. However, marriage to Josh was number
one on her list of interesting topics, so she had trouble
concentrating on the discussion.

Josh. What was she going to do? She'd figured out
Sunday morning, when she'd woken up in his arms,
that she loved him. She hadn't wanted to leave his
embrace.

But she had to. He shouldn't have moved her to
the bed. She'd had to work her anger to fever pitch
to let him know that he'd made a tactical error. She

wasn't a plaything for him to use when he felt like
it.

Without that anger, she would have melted into his
arms and encouraged even more touching from him.
Now he was offering her a permanent place in his
life. Or at least a few years.

But he wasn't offering love.

Which meant she wouldn't be in his bed.

Could she live in the same condo with the man and
not plead for his touch? She didn't know. And that
was what she'd have to decide before she could give
him his answer.

Josh and Will returned almost two hours later.

Kate and Maggie set out leftovers of the meal
they'd shared, and the men ate as if they were starved.
Since it was almost nine o'clock, Maggie wasn't surprised.

She waited until Josh's appetite had been somewhat appeased before she asked the question she already knew the answer to. "Was the condo messed
up?"

"Completely trashed," Josh muttered. "We called
the police, made an insurance report. There wasn't
much else to do."

"Are we going back there tonight?"

"No," Will spoke up. "The front door was
smashed in. I've suggested the three of you stay here.
You need to convince Josh that's what you should
do. Going back to the condo wouldn't be safe. And
it's not easy to stay at a hotel with a baby."

Kate immediately seconded Will's invitation.

Maggie knew they had little choice. But she'd hoped to be alone with Josh and Ginny. It would help her to decide what to do. "I think we should stay here, Josh."

"We'll do what you want."

His polite agreement made her nervous. It was as if he were speaking to a stranger.

"Is Ginny already asleep?" he asked.

"Yes. Do you want to see her?"

He nodded and stood. Maggie got up to take him upstairs, knowing the other two were watching them closely.

Josh followed quietly behind her. When they reached the nursery, he crossed over to the playpen where Ginny was sleeping. Leaning down, he brushed her baby cheek with one finger. Then he took Maggie's arm and left the room.

When the door was closed behind them, he stopped, pulling Maggie to a halt, also. "Do you really want to stay here? I can afford a hotel."

"It will be easier here."

"I'm going to buy a house. I can't afford something this big, but I'll find us a house in a nice neighborhood."

Us? Maggie took a deep breath. "I haven't made up my mind, Josh. I need a little time. But I'll take care of Ginny until—"

"I know you will. But we're a team, Maggie. My plan works. We both care about Ginny. I can give you good financial support while you get your business started. Ginny can have a loving mom. We get along fine. It's perfect."

Maggie tried to remember why she was hesitating. The biggest reason was standing in front of her. She loved him, but he wasn't offering love in return. Would she ever be able to forget him, to forget the upheaval he'd caused in her life? If not, what would she do if she couldn't see him every day?

"Maggie? It will work, I promise," said Josh, leaning toward her.

Taking her heart in her hand, she nodded.

"Yes?" Josh asked, anxiety in his voice.

Did he care? Really care? "Yes," she whispered. Before he could respond, she turned and ran downstairs.

Josh almost lost his balance. He'd begun leaning forward, to seal her agreement with a kiss. But she'd run away.

He followed her down the stairs. Somehow, her answer had been less satisfying than he'd expected. Why? She had agreed to everything he'd offered.

Because I want more than I offered.

He sternly commanded that inner voice to get lost. He didn't want more. A marriage that was basically a business transaction was best. He cared about Maggie, of course. But he wasn't going to give her the power his mother had had over his father.

She wasn't going to disrupt his life.

When he reached the kitchen, he discovered Maggie had told her sister and brother-in-law her decision. Kate glared at him, while Will seemed to be reserving judgment. Great. He and Maggie wouldn't be staying here any longer than they had to, Josh decided.

It was like taking up residence in the middle of a refrigerator.

Maggie had had second, third, fourth, eternal thoughts about whether she'd made the right decision. Yet every day evidence presented itself that she had.

Finding small businesses that needed her services had been ridiculously easy. With the Lucky Charm and Josh's company as her main clients, she'd added enough work from smaller companies to double her income at the accounting firm. Plus, living with Josh as his wife meant her living expenses were taken care of. She could save quite a bit of money.

Most important of all, though, she could be there for Ginny.

Josh, though busy with his work, had spent a lot of hours looking for the perfect house. Maggie had expected him to resist moving, based on the strong statements he'd made when she first came into his life. But he seemed enthusiastic about his decision.

Will had taken some time off from work to accompany Josh on his search, surprising both Kate and Maggie.

"Why do you think Will is going with Josh?" Maggie finally asked her sister on Thursday.

"I don't know. I asked him, but he wouldn't say much."

The men were expected home in a few minutes for dinner, and Maggie checked her watch again. "Josh seems eager to buy a house."

"The man's got the hots for you, sister. And you

thought you should wait until after he bought a house before you married. What did you expect?''

"Kate! Josh hasn't— I mean, this is a marriage of convenience!"

"Does that mean there won't be any sex? Because I can't believe you'll be able to live together without it. He's good-looking, you'll have to admit. And you're not chopped liver yourself," she added, grinning at Maggie.

"Thanks a lot. But I'm not in his league."

"Maggie, think about what you're doing. He'll find sex somewhere. You don't want him sleeping around, do you?"

Maggie closed her eyes. She'd tried not to think about what was going to happen after they married. She wanted Josh. More than she'd thought possible. But she wanted more than just sex.

Besides, since she'd agreed to the marriage, he hadn't touched her. Not even a casual kiss. Or a hug. Nothing. He'd kissed Ginny, hugged *her*. How terrible to be jealous of a baby....

"Maggie?" Josh's voice called from the back door.

Maggie's heart began beating overtime. "Yes?" she called, letting him know she was in the kitchen.

Both men came in from the back door, grinning.

Kate looked at them. "Have a good day?"

"You could say that," Will said.

"In the morning we're going to get the marriage license, and then we'll get married Sunday afternoon," Josh announced, looking quite proud of himself.

"But we weren't going to marry until after you

bought a house," Maggie answered, sounding as if she'd run a race.

"I bought a house this afternoon."

"How soon will you close on it?" She knew it usually took about six weeks.

"Monday. I'm paying cash and it's empty."

"You bought it without having Maggie see it?" Kate asked, her voice rising in outrage.

"It's perfect. She'll love it," Josh insisted. "And we're getting married Sunday."

"You can't plan a wedding in three days," Kate protested again.

"Mother did it in a week, for us," Will reminded his wife.

"That was different. Maggie?" Kate said, staring at her.

"Maggie?" Josh said immediately afterward.

Essentially they were both asking the same question. Was she willing to go along with Josh's plans? But Maggie had already answered the question three days ago, when she'd agreed to marry Josh.

"Yes, of course. I have a cream suit I can wear. We'll get a justice of the peace to marry us." She smiled at her sister's stunned expression. "So, Kate, Monday, you'll be rid of your uninvited house guests."

"Unless she agrees to keep Ginny for a few days so we can have a honeymoon," Josh said calmly.

Maggie whipped around to stare at him. "I don't think a honeymoon will be necessary under the circumstances." If she wore rose-colored glasses, she'd think that the emotion that flashed through Josh's eyes was hurt. But she wasn't that optimistic. "Ginny would be upset."

"Right."

"When do we get to see the house?" Kate asked.

"How about after dinner?" Josh suggested. "I've got the key, the electricity is on so we can turn on the lights, and it's not far away."

The fantasy Josh had been enjoying about his marriage to Maggie shattered when they toured the house. She picked out her bedroom from the five available.

And it wasn't the master bedroom.

She left that room to Josh, choosing instead the one beside Ginny's. Then she asked for the small library off the living room for her office.

A hand came down on his shoulder. "Don't give up," Will whispered. "Kate planned to avoid me when we got married."

Josh frowned at his soon-to-be brother-in-law. "Why would she do that?"

"She was making a marriage of convenience, too. Just like Maggie."

Josh wanted more details, but there was no time to ask for them now. At least Will's words gave him hope. Because he intended to have Maggie in his bed—and sooner rather than later.

Unfortunately, staying at her sister's house, Maggie had managed to avoid any time alone with him, so there'd been no time to talk about ground rules in their coming marriage.

And tonight she'd made it clear what she wanted.

His gaze trailed her lithe form. Since she'd quit her

job at the accounting firm, it seemed to Josh that Maggie was more relaxed. She dressed casually, in jeans that showed off her curves, rather than in outfits like that boxy suit she'd been wearing that first night.

He remembered his first impression of her—that she wasn't terribly attractive. Though he also remembered eyeing her tush as she stomped out of the kitchen. But now, he couldn't imagine any of the women he'd ever dated comparing to Maggie.

She was filled with an incandescent light that radiated from her, and she exuded a caring warmth. Especially when she held Ginny. He wanted her to look at *him* the same way. How sad to be jealous of his own baby....

Three days later Josh stood in Kate and Will's backyard, under the roof of a rented gazebo, waiting for his bride. He'd been introduced to Susan, the third sister, and her half siblings, and also met several old family friends of the O'Connors.

Will's mother, a somewhat pretentious matron, had made a lot of the arrangements, though she was constantly muttering under her breath about rushed weddings.

The three-piece ensemble began playing the wedding march as the back door of the house opened. Josh caught his breath as Maggie stepped outside.

She was wearing a cream suit, as she'd said she would. *And* she was carrying Ginny, dressed in cream also, along with a bouquet of cream roses. Covering Maggie's hair was a small hat with a chin-length veil. A matching bow sat atop Ginny's dark curls.

His two beautiful ladies.

Josh's heart swelled with pride as they stepped to his side. He reached for Maggie's hand, noticing how adept she'd become at handling Ginny in the past two weeks.

The judge Will had invited to perform the ceremony cleared his throat and began those momentous words Josh had never thought to hear again. But there was no panic in his heart, as he'd expected.

He could trust Maggie. He knew that. And besides, he wasn't going to love her. He fully intended to *make love* to her, but he wasn't going to love her.

And then the judge asked him to do just that.

Maggie stared at the beautiful diamond band Josh had surprised her with only four hours ago. She was Mrs. Joshua McKinley.

She sighed.

It hadn't been as wonderful as she'd expected. It wasn't the wedding ceremony that had disappointed her. Kate's mother-in-law, with Kate's assistance, had done a great job. And the food, from the Lucky Charm Diner, of course, had been delicious.

It was the emotions that filled her, the ones she read on Josh's face that disturbed her. He'd given her exactly what he'd offered. A marriage of convenience.

"Foolish girl. What did you expect?" she asked herself as she tucked Ginny into bed upstairs at Kate and Will's.

Silly question. She knew what she'd hoped for. But the closer they came to the wedding, the more distant

Josh had grown. She'd discovered he'd been married before, but it clearly had been an unhappy union.

It doesn't matter, she assured herself. After all, they had a business arrangement, so no one was expecting happily ever after. They'd be just fine.

As long as she could forget the longings that filled her. And she'd have to, because Josh hadn't shown any interest in loving her.

She returned downstairs and discovered Kate and Will standing by the front door with a suitcase.

"What's going on?" she asked, puzzled.

"We decided to have Angie stay overnight to take care of the babies. And Will and I are going to the Plaza Hotel for the night." Kate didn't look terribly happy about their decision.

"You don't seem pleased about going, Kate," Maggie noted slowly, trying to figure out what was going on.

"It was Will's idea," Kate muttered.

"I'm a romantic fool," Will murmured, a grin on his face. "Since Nate was born, we haven't had a single uninterrupted night."

"That's not true!" Kate protested. "Remember—"

Will stopped her by covering her lips with his and pulling her into a passionate embrace.

Maggie's heart ached with jealousy. She wanted her husband to treat her in the same manner.

"Maggie?" Josh called from the hallway behind her. "Did Ginny go to sleep okay?"

"Yes," she assured him, somewhat breathless. "She's already asleep."

Will stopped kissing his wife and said goodbye, sweeping her out the door before the other two could respond.

"They…they're going to a hotel."

"Yeah, Will told me."

Maggie stood across from him, unable to think of a thing to say.

"Come on. There's a good movie on television." He turned and walked into the den without waiting for her.

Not knowing what else to do, she followed him.

Two hours later the movie ended. And the couple who'd entered the room still remained separated by about three feet of sofa cushions.

Several times Josh had initiated a conversation, but it always fizzled out. Maggie didn't know what he was trying to say, but whatever it was never got said.

Finally, they walked up the stairs together, but, like every other night since they'd moved into Kate and Will's house, Maggie entered the small bedroom next to the nursery.

"Good night, Josh," she said hurriedly, afraid if she didn't separate from him quickly, she'd throw herself in his arms and beg him to make love to her.

Closing the door when he didn't respond, she leaned against it, thinking that at least Kate and Will would have a romantic night.

Because the bride and groom sure weren't going to.

Chapter Ten

The next week was hectic.

Not only did Maggie's belongings have to be packed and moved, but the shambles of Josh's condo had to be sorted out, as well. Then they had to shop to replace items that had been destroyed. Like a television set, dishes, a breakfast table.

The goons who'd broken in had taken out their frustration on most of Josh's possessions.

Maggie and Josh didn't actually move into the house until Tuesday. The day when Maggie's bedroom furniture was moved in, along with Josh's king-size bed.

Into separate rooms, of course.

Josh considered speaking to Maggie before the beds arrived. It was ridiculous to think they could live in the same house, married to each other, and sleep in separate rooms.

But Maggie had given him no indication that separate beds bothered her.

"Josh?" she called from her room, shaking him from his depressing thoughts.

"Yeah?" he answered as he left the master bedroom and walked down the hall to her room.

"I've got some extra pillows. Do you need any of them?" She was bent over her bed, smoothing the coverlet.

"No, thank you. I have plenty of pillows."

"Even after they slashed several?"

"Yeah." Pillows weren't what he needed in his bedroom.

Her back was turned to him and his gaze lovingly outlined her hips as he wished his hands could do. When she turned, his face was burning. He felt as if he'd been caught reading a racy magazine, something he hadn't done since puberty.

"I really appreciate your working half days this week, so we can get settled in. It's a beautiful house."

"I'm glad you like it. Mrs. Lassiter, my cleaning lady, has agreed to come a couple of days a week to help out. She'll be here tomorrow."

"Two days a week? Can you afford that?" She looked anxious. Before Josh could reassure her, she said, "I can pay half. I think my business is going to be quite prosperous."

He felt as if she'd insulted him. "I can pay my own way, Maggie."

Her eyebrows rose, drawing his attention to her hazel eyes. "You shouldn't have to pay my way, too, Josh. Not completely."

"That was our agreement. You're going to be taking care of Ginny *and* working. I don't want you to feel like a servant." He wanted her to feel like a wife. A wife who slept in her husband's bed.

She seemed taken aback by his harsh tone. "You're taking care of Ginny, too. You're the one who put her down for her afternoon nap."

"I was here. After this week, I'll need to put in more hours. I have a business to run."

He hadn't meant to sound so gruff, but she had to understand. The warmth in her gaze disappeared, and he felt sure she was disappointed by his response. She probably wanted him to change jobs. Like his mother. Like his first wife.

He turned and stalked out of her bedroom. He couldn't stay there without wanting to take her to bed. Maybe separate bedrooms was a good idea, because he couldn't seem to control himself around her.

She hadn't touched him since he'd offered marriage.

Their marriage was a disaster.

Maggie watched Josh leave her bedroom, a frown on his face. Nothing she did or said seemed to make him happy. Only Ginny brought out his smiles.

With a sigh, she went back downstairs to the kitchen. The house was beautiful. She couldn't have chosen better, but it didn't matter. It wasn't going to become a home unless things changed.

It was hard to appear natural around Josh, when desire surged through her veins every time she got within sight of him. A rather new experience for her, the almost overpowering need that filled her.

Other than her raging hormones, everything was working well. She tended to her business in the afternoon while Josh was home, and sometimes in the mornings when Ginny played in her playpen. With Mrs. Lassiter coming two days a week, the housework would be manageable.

All she had to worry about was feeding her little family.

Gathering the ingredients for the chicken casserole she intended to make for dinner, Maggie was concentrating on the recipe until Josh entered the kitchen.

"I have to go out. Pete called and there's a problem."

"All right. Will you be back for dinner?"

Her question appeared to irritate him.

"I don't know, Maggie. I'll have to play it by ear."

"If I'm asleep, I'll leave dinner in the refrigerator," she said, hiding her emotions. It wasn't that she minded eating dinner alone. She was used to that. But she worried that Josh might get hurt.

"Thanks." He turned and headed for the garage.

Though she warned herself she should say nothing else, she couldn't remain quiet. "Josh?"

"Yeah?" He sounded wary.

"Be careful."

He turned and frowned at her. "Maggie, I told you my work isn't that dangerous. Last week was the first time—"

"I know," she said hurriedly, her smile wobbly,

trying to assure him she wasn't a weak, demanding woman. "Just...be careful."

Something in his expression changed, and he walked back to her. Much to her surprise, considering the past week, he took hold of her upper arms and tugged her toward him. "You be careful, too. Lots of accidents happen in the home."

His reversal of concern tickled her, and she relaxed for the first time in days. "Oh, yes, those dreadful pots and pans can attack when you're least expecting them," she teased with a chuckle.

He grinned. Then he pulled her closer and kissed her.

Before Maggie could think, her arms circled his neck and she leaned into his hard body, opening her mouth to him. He took full advantage, taking her breath away. When he lifted his head, she could barely stand.

"I'll hurry back," he promised huskily, before he stepped back and hurried out the door.

"Oh, my," Maggie muttered to herself.

She'd decided she could live with Josh and not expect anything more than friendship. But that kiss had just shot her theory to bits.

He was such a wonderful man. He could have any woman he wanted, she knew. After all, he was handsome, intelligent, caring and financially solvent. And she wanted all of him for herself.

But that hadn't been his plan. All he'd offered was friendship. So what was she going to do now?

"You'll forget," she ordered herself. "He thought you wanted him to kiss you. He probably thought you were begging. Really, Maggie, you must control your-self.''

Her self-lecture didn't dismiss the hunger she felt for Josh McKinley. Maybe the chicken casserole would do the job. But she sure didn't think so.

He'd been an idiot!

Josh berated himself all the way home.

First of all he shouldn't have kissed her. Because it only made him want to kiss her again. Real bad.

And then, he'd tricked her. He could've told her Pete's problem was with the computer. Instead, he'd let her think he was taking on the entire criminal world.

But the concern in her gaze had been so sweet.

Almost as sweet as the taste of her lips.

Man, if he could get so worked up kissing her, what control would he have if he took her to bed? Just imagining her naked, her smooth skin inviting his touch, her arms held out in encouragement, her luscious lips smiling, caused a definite reaction.

He shifted in the car seat. His jeans were too tight. That bulge had better disappear before he entered the house. Maggie would notice at once and be disgusted with him.

After all, if she'd wanted him, she would've let him know by now. It wouldn't take a rocket scientist to know that he would accept any kind of invitation without any hesitation.

He pushed the garage door opener and eased the Jeep in the garage. At least he wouldn't have to worry about facing her tonight. It was after one o'clock. She'd be asleep.

He unlocked the back door and crept across the tile to the kitchen. She'd left the light on for him. He pushed the swinging door open, then came to an abrupt halt.

"Maggie! What are you doing up? Is Ginny sick?"

She'd been reading a book, which she now shut. "No. I wasn't sleepy and thought I'd wait for you. Actually, I hadn't realized it was so late. I was just going to go upstairs."

Her sleepy smile made him think of beds, sheets, slick bodies, sex. He turned away and opened the refrigerator. He needed something cold. In a hurry.

"Well, don't let me keep you."

"It's okay. I'll heat some of the casserole for you."

Damn, if she didn't get out of the kitchen, she'd see his arousal. "No, thanks, I'm not hungry."

"But, Josh, you have to eat something. Skipping meals isn't good for you."

"Pete and I ordered a pizza. I'm not hungry." He knew his tone was harsh, but he was desperate. He couldn't even turn around until she cleared out. Her voice alone, sexy velvet, husky honey, sent shivers all over him.

"Oh."

Just one soft sound. Filled with disappointment.

Without thinking, he whirled around. "Maggie, I didn't mean— You shouldn't have—"

"It's okay. I didn't realize you'd get a chance to eat." She'd gotten up and turned toward the door, her shoulders slumped.

"Sweetheart, wait," he called and hurried after her. He couldn't let her think he didn't appreciate her efforts. "I should've called to tell you, but we didn't order the pizza until almost midnight, and I thought you'd be asleep."

She turned just as he reached her, and she was practically in his embrace without his intending to touch her. The smile, that warm, butter-melting smile she had lately reserved just for Ginny, lit her face.

His hands gathered her to him. Reflex action, that was all. He wasn't going to take advantage of her. Of course he wasn't.

But she leaned into him, as she had earlier when he'd kissed her. Damn, didn't she have any self-preservation instincts? He wasn't going to be able to resist her much longer. In fact, she'd have to be a child not to recognize his arousal when they were touching from shoulder to knee.

"Maggie, you'd better go to bed."

The light went out of her smile. "Yes, of course. Good night."

She shoved against his chest, but he didn't release her. He told his hands to pull back. They did, but they pulled Maggie with them. Tricky hands.

Her gaze returned to his face, a question in it.

The only answer he had for her brought on more questions. But he couldn't have resisted her lips at that moment even if she were cursing him.

She didn't resist him, either.

His heart thudded as her soft lips molded to his, opened to him, inviting him to come even closer to her sweetness. "Oh, Maggie," he muttered as his lips left hers to trace a path down her delicate neck. He breathed in the soft scent of her hair, and his hands roamed her back, stroking and caressing every inch of her.

Somewhere in that embrace, he realized she wasn't wearing a bra. He jerked back, frowning.

"Is something wrong?" she whispered, scanning his face anxiously.

"You're not wearing a bra!" he exclaimed, regretting that he sounded so accusatory.

She seemed surprised by his words. "I'm wearing my pajamas. I don't wear a bra to bed."

He gulped and took several steps back, afraid if he didn't send her away at once, he'd take her on the kitchen floor. "Go to bed, Maggie."

"I have to go to bed because I'm not wearing a bra?" She sounded confused.

"Damn it, yes! I can't control myself much longer. Unless you want to continue this…this—" he couldn't think of what to call their kissing "—you'd better go to your room and lock your door."

"There's no lock on my door."

He stared at her, unable to believe she'd said those words so calmly, with no fear, no alarm. What was wrong with her?

"Maggie, I can't be responsible—"

"I don't think I want you to be."

It took a moment for her whispered words to sink in. When they did, he closed the distance between them so quickly she didn't have a chance to get away.

Touching her again, he ground his teeth, then muttered, "When will you be sure?"

Just as he'd imagined, her lips spread in a soft, welcoming smile.

"Maggie?" he whispered, at the end of his restraint.

"Let's go upstairs," she suggested, and held out a hand.

As he'd dreamed.

He took her hand and raced up the stairs. Heading down the hall to the master bedroom, he came to an abrupt halt when Maggie stopped. Had she changed her mind?

"Could we— I'd like to...to use my bed. Do you mind?"

"Sweetheart, I'm willing to use whatever you want. As long as you let me love you." The wall, the floor, the kitchen table, whatever.

She smiled again, this time with flushed cheeks, and opened the door to her room.

He stood on the threshold, watching her move toward the bed. Was he dreaming? He'd wanted an invitation to her bed, but he hadn't expected one. She hadn't shown any interest in making love. What had changed?

"Maggie?" What kind of idiot was he, questioning her? He could bury himself in her, find relief for the desire that had made his life miserable almost from the first of his days—and nights—spent with Maggie.

"Yes?" she asked as she turned, still smiling. When she noticed he was hovering at the door, the smile disappeared. "What's wrong?"

"I just want to be sure. You don't have to do this."

Her face tensed, her eyes going blank. "I...I know."

Tense silence filled the room, and Josh didn't know where to look. He certainly couldn't stare at Maggie, or he'd forget what he'd just said.

"If...if you're not interested—"

"Hell, Maggie, I'm interested!" he exploded, then added more quietly, "But this wasn't part of the agreement."

Her spine stiffened and Josh prepared himself for her rejection, knowing he'd spend the rest of the night trying to recover if she sent him away.

"I want it to be a part of the agreement."

Her whispered words took time to penetrate his befuddled brain. When he finally realized what she'd said, he gasped. "You're saying yes?"

She nodded.

Well, he'd done the noble thing. He'd held himself in check, given her a chance to reconsider. Taking the first step, he reached out for her. As he grabbed her waist and hauled her up against him, her arms slid around his neck, and she tilted her lips toward his.

His mouth settled over hers, his tongue seeking entry at once, looking for her sweet taste, finding Maggie more than cooperative. Damn, why had they wasted so much time?

He kissed her again and again, unable to slake his thirst. When he moved them closer to the bed, she pulled back. "The door. Close the door."

When he turned back from the closed door, he discovered Maggie had moved to the bed and was waiting for him. He joined her, his mouth returning to hers, but his hands sped to the buttons on her simple cotton pajamas. Her hands slid beneath his polo shirt and massaged his chest, sending shivers through him.

He ripped the rest of the buttons free and bared her breasts. Lifting his mouth from hers, he stared at their rounded beauty, topped by tight buds. His mouth swooped to first one and then the other, leaving them wet from his loving.

A moan from Maggie drew his mouth back to hers. Their tongues mated and withdrew, then repeated the electrifying touch. His breathing sped up and he had to break away to gasp oxygen.

She shoved at his shirt and he whipped it off before he returned to spread out atop her, his hands shoving down her pajama bottoms. He discovered pale pink bikini panties guarding his goal.

Then he was distracted by Maggie's hands at the top button on his jeans. He almost exploded, just thinking about her touching him. He might not even last long enough to consummate their lovemaking.

"Easy, baby, easy," he whispered.

"I want—" she began, but he covered her mouth again.

He didn't need to hear the words. Her body thrummed with electricity, as did his. Sex had never been like this before.

Inserting his hand inside that pink scrap of material, he felt her readiness as her frantic hands tugged at his shoulders and her legs widened in invitation. He broke off the kiss and reached for the top button on his jeans.

Maggie ground against his leg, and he wanted to

be inside her, to feel that movement, to know he was satisfying her. His fingers seemed to be all thumbs as he tried to free himself.

"Josh," she whispered, her hands returning to his chest, raking through his chest hairs, reaching around him, pulling, caressing, urging him.

He managed to shuck his jeans and briefs until they reached his ankles, where he encountered his tennis shoes. He'd forgotten he still wore them. With a muttered curse, he yanked on the shoelaces of his right shoe and broke them, scraping the shoe off. The second one came untied more easily, and he was able to finish undressing and return to Maggie's eager body.

Their lips joined, and his blood raced faster and faster. He moved between her legs and let his arousal settle there, poised, ready, as he checked one more time to be sure she was ready for him.

Then he plunged into her.

And felt her convulsive jerk of pain.

His eyes widened in shock as he realized she was a virgin. Stunned, worried, he didn't move, frantically wondering what he should do. He could withdraw, he thought, hoped, but—

Before he could make that decision, Maggie's hands clutched his shoulders and urged him toward her.

"Josh, don't—"

With painful determination, he returned to her lips, to soothe, caress, excite. He wanted her first time to be the best experience he could make it. Soon they were both so caught up in sensations, it was impossible to think.

When they reached satisfaction together, their bodies sweat-slicked and sated, he collapsed against her. Then his mind kicked in again, and he felt shame fill him. He'd ripped into her as if she'd been experienced.

He'd hurt her.

"Maggie," he whispered, his voice strained. "I'm sorry. I'm so sorry."

She stilled beneath him, not even seeming to breathe.

"Maggie? Are you all right?"

He pushed up so he could see her face. Her eyes were closed, her cheeks deathly pale, and tears trickled down her face.

Chapter Eleven

"Please leave," Maggie whispered, keeping her eyes closed. It would be too painful to see the displeasure on his beloved face.

"Maggie—"

"Please."

She felt him withdraw, felt her skin cool as he moved away. She clawed for the covers and turned her back to him. Shame filled her. She'd begged him to make love to her. And she'd disappointed him.

She'd never considered herself a beauty, but she'd thought she and Josh might connect physically. Her desire for him hadn't been enough, however.

He'd apologized.

Perhaps she should've been the one to apologize. Her inexperience had betrayed her. She didn't know how to please her husband.

"Maggie, I'm...I'm sorry."

She didn't move or acknowledge his words in any way.

Though, if he said them again, she thought she might scream and scratch his eyes out. She didn't want his apologies. She wanted his love.

But that was not to be.

The door closed, and she released her pent-up breath, her body sinking into the mattress. She'd be sore in the morning, both because of their lovemaking and because of the tension that filled her.

Until Josh's apology, she'd been exhilarated, her blood pumping with pleasure, unbelievable pleasure. She'd never experienced anything as moving, as completing. Or as soul-destroying when she realized her husband...Josh...had not been similarly moved.

The tears continued to flow, and she sobbed into her pillow. From heaven to hell in such a brief spate of time.

What was she going to do now?

She'd hoped for the fairy-tale ending, for happily ever after, for what Kate had. Maggie had a husband, a baby, a beautiful house.

But her husband didn't love her.

He didn't even want her. She remembered now how reluctantly he'd stood on her bedroom threshold, asking her again if she wanted him to make love to her. She'd had to plead with him.

How humiliating.

It was several hours before Maggie managed to fall asleep. Miserable hours spent castigating herself for her shortfalls.

* * *

Josh heard Maggie get up with Ginny around six o'clock. He wanted to join her, to help with his child, but he didn't dare. He feared his presence would only make things worse.

What was he going to do now?

He assured himself one more time that he hadn't raped Maggie. He knew that. But as he relived their glorious lovemaking to the point of his entry, he swallowed hard. He felt again her pain at his careless treatment.

But he hadn't known!

Why hadn't she told him? She was twenty-six. Most women were experienced by that age. It had never occurred to him that she wouldn't be.

He ignored the sneaky feeling of satisfaction that he'd been Maggie's first lover. If he'd known, he'd have been a considerate lover, initiating her into the rigors of the greatest sharing on earth.

But he hadn't known.

Would she forgive him? Would she allow him to show her how wonderful lovemaking could be between two people as ideally suited to each other as they were? He couldn't believe how far over the top she'd taken him. It hadn't been *his* first time. But it had felt like it.

If only he'd known.

After a half hour of hearing no movement, he rolled from his bed and hit the shower. He figured it would be better to be up and out of there before Maggie came downstairs. He needed to give her time. No man would try to discuss his sex life over breakfast.

Maybe he'd make reservations at a romantic, candlelit restaurant. Court her. Let her know he—

Damn! He loved Maggie.

Panic filled him. He hadn't intended to love her. She was wonderful, of course, but he didn't want to make himself vulnerable. He stood under the stream of water, swallowing convulsively.

Could he stop loving her?

No time was necessary to answer that question. No, he couldn't stop loving her.

He shut off the water and stepped out of the shower. Grabbing a towel, he roughly dried his body, trying to ignore his response to the thought of loving Maggie.

With a determination that pleased him, he realized he would fight for Maggie, for their love, their family. He'd convince her to love him. She'd at least wanted him last night. That was a start.

If she ever let him come within a mile of her again.

Maggie had taken Ginny into her bed after Ginny's morning bottle, and the two of them slept for three more hours.

She knew why *she* slept—she hadn't gotten much sleep last night. But she didn't understand why Ginny was so sleepy. The baby babbled at her now, but she seemed cranky. Maggie felt her forehead and gasped.

The baby was hot.

Immediately, after checking her watch, Maggie called the diner and asked for Kate. Her misery and despair were forgotten as she worried over Ginny.

"Kate, Ginny's hot! I think she's running a fever."

JUDY CHRISTENBERRY 155

"Maggie? Calm down. Babies do that. Is she cutting a tooth?"

"I don't know." She tried to look into Ginny's mouth, but the baby fussed and pulled away. "I can't see anything. She's got two front teeth already."

"Put your finger in her mouth and run it over her gums. See if you can feel a break in the skin."

Maggie wasn't sure she would be able to identify a break in the skin, but she followed her sister's directions. When she felt the barest edge of a little tooth on the bottom gum, she felt as if she'd discovered gold.

"Yes! Yes, she does. I mean, there is a break. Is that the reason she's running a fever?"

"Yes. Just give her some baby aspirin and lots of water. She'll be all right."

"What kind of baby aspirin?"

"You don't have any there?"

"No, but I'll go get some."

"Is Josh there? Send him," Kate suggested.

"No, he's gone to work." At least she hoped and prayed he had. She couldn't face him this morning.

"Then sit tight. I'll go get the aspirin for you. See you in a few minutes." Kate hung up before Maggie could protest.

She felt bad. Kate had a busy schedule and didn't have time to run errands for Maggie. But she also felt a sense of relief. At least she had Kate, family, to support her. And Susan, too.

Even though Josh didn't love her, want her, she had a family.

Her pleasure faded as she thought of her husband,

longing to feel his arms around her, to hear him whisper her name.

By the time Kate arrived, Maggie was so depressed, she burst into tears.

"Maggie, really, the baby's not that sick. She's just teething."

Maggie plopped down in a kitchen chair, Ginny clutched against her breasts. "It's not Ginny. It's me!"

Midway through the morning Josh called a florist and ordered a dozen red roses sent to his house. When he hung up the phone, he discovered Pete staring at him.

"What?"

"You in trouble already? You've only been married less than a week."

"I'm sending the roses because I love my wife," he stated emphatically, amazed at how he enjoyed saying those words, when he'd once thought loving a woman would be the kiss of death.

"Yeah, right," Pete replied with a sarcastic grin. "That's what they all say."

"Okay, so maybe I messed up a little. But I didn't intend to." He hadn't. But he couldn't promise, even to himself, to back off, give Maggie time. He wanted her right now so badly he didn't think he could stand up without advertising that fact.

He now understood the real reason for a honeymoon. It gave a man a chance to make love to his wife without the rest of the world knowing how oversexed he was. The thought of occupying a hotel room with Maggie for a week or two was so thrilling, he knew he wouldn't emerge until he had to return home.

"Maybe you'd better move right on up the ladder to diamonds. They're more effective than roses."

"Diamonds?" Josh considered, willing to try anything.

"Hey, I was only kidding. Unless whatever you did was worse than you admitted." Pete studied him closely.

"No! No, it wasn't. Just…just a minor thing." One that would haunt him until he could erase its memory by making love to Maggie again. With tenderness and consideration.

His secretary interrupted his worrying. "Josh, Soquatch Insurance is on line two."

"Insurance?" He looked at Pete. "Do we have a case with them?" His firm was frequently hired to check out claims.

"Nope. Not unless Don took it on yesterday."

Josh picked up the phone. "This is Josh McKinley."

Half an hour later, he hung up the phone, a broad smile on his face. "Well, Pete, we've struck the mother lode."

"What are you talking about?"

"Soquatch Insurance Company is one of the largest employers in Kansas City. They've just hired us to do background checks on every person they employ and any new people they take on. And they're paying top rate."

"Wow. That's a great haul. Are we going to be able to handle that much business?"

"We are as soon as I hire a couple of new people. Most of the work will be over the computer, however. Only if there's a red flag in the research will we actually have to check it out in person."

Pete frowned. "Computer work? That's not very exciting."

A feeling that had been growing in Josh crystallized at that moment. "You know, I enjoy working on the computer. And with my family, now, I think I might appreciate more regular hours. You and Don still seem to enjoy the chase, but I think I'm ready to pull back a little."

"Man, I never thought I'd hear you say that," Pete exclaimed, amazement on his face.

"I didn't, either," Josh assured him, but in his mind he was thinking of Maggie and Ginny waiting at home for him. He didn't want to be away from them any more than he had to be. In fact, he might set up an office in the house and work there some days.

The best of both worlds.

He immediately began searching for possible candidates to expand his firm. And free him up for a more traditional family life.

Strangely enough, he was looking forward to it.

Once Ginny took the aspirin and had her lunch, she was ready for her afternoon nap. Mrs. Lassiter promised to watch over her as she cleaned, and Maggie was being dragged off to the Lucky Charm Diner by Kate for a late lunch. And a consultation.

When they arrived, Susan, their half sister, whom

Kate had summoned by phone, was waiting for them in the last booth, the one the family used.

"What's so urgent?" Susan asked as Kate and Maggie slid in across from her.

Maggie's cheeks flamed and she stared down at the tabletop. It was embarrassing to explain her problem.

Kate seemed to have no difficulty. "Maggie's fallen in love with Josh, but she doesn't think he loves her."

"But I thought he— Well, everything did happen quickly," Susan finished tactfully.

Kate rolled her eyes and laughed, but Maggie sent Susan a grateful smile. "Yes, it did. I guess I'm expecting miracles."

"Miracles are nice," Susan agreed. When silence fell, she looked at Kate. Though she'd only known her sisters a short while, she knew what was coming. "You have a plan?"

Kate chuckled. "You've learned to read us quickly, haven't you? Yes, I have a plan. Maggie thinks she should be patient, give him time. *I* think she should knock his socks off."

"How?"

"Maggie's always downplayed her looks. She dresses like someone's maiden aunt, but her figure is just as good as mine, or yours, for that matter. Since you're the most stylish of the three of us, I thought you could show her what to do."

"You mean how to dress to attract men? I don't—"

"Susan, sweetie, I know you don't set out to flirt, but men notice you."

"Because she's so pretty, Kate. I'm not like either one of you," Maggie protested. "You're a redhead who sparks electricity, and Susan is a blonde, every man's dream. I'm just…me."

"See what I mean?" Kate said, raising her hands, palms up, in surrender.

"Yes, I think I do. It'll take a little time and money, Maggie. Do you have some spare money for a new wardrobe?" Susan asked. Money always had to be a consideration in her decisions.

"Yes, I—"

"I do, if she doesn't. It can be a wedding present," Kate added as Maggie opened her mouth to protest.

"I have savings, Kate. You know that. I'm perfectly willing to spend my savings to attract Josh's attention." She flirted with the mental image of herself as a siren, but she couldn't quite bring the picture into focus. "Susan, are you sure anything can be done?"

Susan looked at Maggie first, then Kate. Maggie stared as the other two burst into laughter.

Finally Susan sobered. "Maggie, when was the last time you had a good haircut? You always just scrape it back. And how much makeup are you wearing? My guess would be none. Have you ever pampered yourself with a massage? How old are those baggy jeans you're wearing? What are your best colors?" She stopped as Maggie held up a hand.

"Okay, okay, I get the picture, but I don't want to trick Josh into loving me. I don't want to hide myself. If he can't love the real me, then—"

Kate slipped an arm around her. "Maggie, anyone

would love the real you. But men sometimes forget to look beneath the surface. Susan's not going to change the real you. She's just going to add a little polish.''

Maggie drew a deep breath. "Okay. When?"

"Can it wait until Saturday? I really can't get away from work until then," Susan explained.

Maggie thought about the intervening days. It was only Wednesday. She'd have to face Josh for three more days, with her humiliation fresh on her mind.

But three days was nothing compared to the rest of her life. If Josh didn't decide to leave her in that time, she could wait.

"I think so."

Susan frowned. "Are you that worried? I could take a vacation day, I suppose, but I was saving it until school's out." She was raising her two half siblings on her own.

"No, that's not necessary," Maggie hurriedly assured her, ashamed of herself.

"Great. Then we'll meet early Saturday morning and get started. Can Josh take care of Ginny all day?" Kate asked.

"Yes," Maggie agreed with a firm nod. She'd insist.

"Then Saturday is B-day, beautification of Maggie day," Susan agreed. "I'll set up the appointments."

Josh arrived home at five on the dot. He'd called earlier in the day, but Mrs. Lassiter had answered the phone and told him Maggie had gone out with Kate. His roses had arrived while she was gone.

The house seemed silent as he entered, but he'd noted Maggie's car in the garage. She should be here unless she was still out with Kate. But Mrs. Lassiter was gone, so someone had to be taking care of Ginny.

"Maggie?"

He didn't hear an answer. A quick search of the downstairs revealed nothing, and he rushed up the stairs, panic starting to grow. "Maggie?"

"I'm in Ginny's room," she called.

He reached the baby's room almost out of breath. Maggie was bent over the baby bed, changing Ginny's diaper.

"Hi, how are my girls?" he asked, keeping his voice cheerful. He'd decided the best approach was to pretend last night hadn't happened.

"Fine. Would you play with Ginny while I begin dinner?"

She was almost past him and out the door when he collected himself. Afraid to touch her, not knowing how she'd react, he said, "Wait. I thought I'd take us out to dinner. I had some good news today, and I thought we'd celebrate."

"I don't think Ginny will feel like it. She's teething," she said calmly and entered the hallway.

"We'll get a sitter," he called after her. In truth, he hadn't intended Ginny to go. Not to a romantic restaurant for a candlelight dinner.

"I don't think I should leave her. She's not feeling well." She never even broke step.

Ginny began fussing, and he turned back into the nursery. "Hello, angel. I missed you today," he whispered, picking her up in his arms and cuddling her.

"I missed your new mommy, too, but I don't think she missed me. She didn't even ask about my big news. Or say anything about the roses."

After about fifteen minutes in the nursery, Josh got the brilliant idea that he and Ginny should join Maggie in the kitchen. He settled himself and the baby at the table, waiting for Maggie to notice them.

She did. In a matter of seconds, she'd tied a bib on Ginny, where she sat in the high chair, and put several jars of baby food in front of Josh.

"You don't mind feeding Ginny, do you?"

"No, of course not." He noticed her gaze never met his, and she avoided coming into contact with him.

"You didn't ask about my big news." He gave Ginny a bite of carrots before he looked at Maggie.

She was staring at him, but she hurriedly turned away as soon as he looked up. "Sorry. What was it?"

He told her of the insurance company's call and what it would mean. "I'll be working at the office more, doing computer searches, instead of going out. It will mean more regular hours. And I may even be able to work from home some days."

She kept her head bent over the pot on the stove, stirring whatever was in there as if her life depended on it. "Are you sure you'll like the change? I thought you enjoyed the...the excitement of your job."

"I'm not as young as I used to be. Besides, now I have a family." He'd meant to convey his willingness to spend more time with her and Ginny. Somehow, he didn't think she saw it that way.

"No one asked you to change!" she snapped, her cheeks flushed.

"But, Maggie—"

She poured the contents of the pan into a bowl and set it down in front of him. "I said I'd take care of Ginny." Then she snatched a salad from the refrigerator and put it in front of him. Lifting Ginny from the high chair, she reached into the refrigerator and plucked a full bottle from it.

"I'm going upstairs to feed Ginny her bottle."

"What about your dinner?" He'd planned to talk to her while they ate, hopefully in a relaxed atmosphere.

"I'm not hungry."

She and the baby left the kitchen, and Josh stared at his dinner. He didn't want food, either. He wanted Maggie. But it looked like he was going to have to work harder at apologizing before he got a chance to get close to her.

Chapter Twelve

The next two days frustrated Josh. Every time he entered a room with Maggie in it, she left. She'd offered a polite smile as she thanked him for the roses, but that had been the last time she'd smiled at him.

Or looked at him.

And other than polite utterances, she never talked to him.

He debated his choices. Finally he decided Saturday would be the day he forced her to discuss what had happened between them. Because he couldn't go much longer without touching her.

When he woke up Saturday morning, he eagerly showered and rushed downstairs. He had to clear things up with Maggie because he couldn't concentrate on anything.

And he wanted to make love to her again.

She was already downstairs in the kitchen, with Ginny in her high chair. When he entered the kitchen, he paused in the doorway, to be sure he blocked any possible exit.

Instead of trying to leave, she set a full plate of eggs and bacon in front of his usual seat and turned back to the stove. Did she have radar? How did she know he would be down now?

"Thanks, Maggie. How'd you know I'd—"

"I heard the shower."

"Well, thank you. You didn't need to fix my breakfast, but it looks good."

As if he hadn't spoken, she said, "I have to go out today. I hope you can take care of Ginny. If you have difficulty, you can call Angie, Kate's nanny."

"You're going out?" That didn't fit in with his plans.

"Yes. I'm going somewhere with Kate and Susan."

"For the entire day?"

"Yes."

"Maggie, I wanted us to talk today."

She stopped rinsing dishes, but she didn't turn to look at him. Finally she resumed her cleaning. "What about?"

"You know what about." He wasn't going to let her get away with pretending she didn't know. "I'm talking about what happened Tuesday night."

"I don't want to talk about it."

"Well, I do. You won't even look at me, much less…anything else. We've got to discuss what happened."

"You've already apologized. It wasn't your fault,

anyway, so I don't see that there's anything else to be said.''

"But I didn't intend—"

"I know you didn't." She wiped her hands at the sink and came toward him.

His heart started pumping faster. Maybe she'd reach out and touch him now, let him feel her soft, warm skin on his, offer a conciliatory kiss.

Instead she reached for Ginny. "I'll go change Ginny's diaper before I leave."

"I can do that," he protested, wanting her to stay near him.

She ignored him and left the room, a talent she'd perfected the past few days.

Unable to eat, he jumped to his feet and paced the kitchen, trying to decide what to do. Was she going to avoid him forever? She said she didn't blame him for what had happened, but if that was true, why was she still treating him like a leper?

He knew now how inexperienced she was. He wouldn't treat her so carelessly in the future. He'd be careful, tender, loving…his body responded to such thoughts.

Hearing Maggie come back down the stairs, he hurriedly sat down at the table again, to cover his reaction.

"Ginny's bottles are in the refrigerator. There's a list on the counter of what you should feed her for lunch. If she gets feverish, the baby aspirin is on the shelf.''

"When will you be back?"

"I don't know. Probably around six. If I'm going to be later, I'll call."

She put Ginny in the high chair beside him, but he caught her wrist before she could get away.

"Maggie, we still need to talk."

He didn't understand the panic-stricken look on her face, which she quickly hid. Staring down at their hands, she said in a whisper, "Just give me today, Josh."

"Of course I'll give you today, Maggie, but—"

"Thank you," she said, and tugged at his hold.

He could swear she was on the verge of tears. Though he released her wrist, he rose at the same time and enfolded her in his arms. "I'll be waiting for you to come home." Then he lowered his mouth to hers and kissed her. Hunger rocked him so hard, he had to force himself to release her.

After a stunned look at him, she rushed out the door.

It was going to be a long day.

"I think Josh is going to—going to tell me he's leaving me," Maggie confessed to her sisters as they drove to their first appointment.

"Why do you say that?" Kate demanded.

"He said we had to talk tonight."

Susan stared at her. "Married couples are supposed to talk, Maggie. Why would that make you think he's going to ask for a divorce?"

"Because of Tuesday night," Maggie answered automatically, forgetting that Susan didn't know about that event. Maggie was concentrating on remembering the kiss she and Josh had exchanged just before she left.

It had only increased the hunger she felt for him, for his kisses, his embraces, his love. Maybe he wanted to torture her, to show her what she couldn't have. Or maybe, she thought, willing to take care of the torture all by herself, he wanted to try again.

She closed her eyes in silent prayer.

"Maggie? What happened Tuesday night?"

Maggie's eyes popped open. "Uh, um, we...we made love."

Susan's eyes widened and then her mouth rounded into an *Oh*. "I thought it was a marriage of convenience."

"It was. It is. I mean—it just happened."

"But if you want a real marriage, why is that bad?"

Kate chuckled. "You sound confused, Susan."

"I am. Explain, Maggie."

"He apologized afterward." Maggie heard his appalled tones over and over again.

"Oh. What was he apologizing for?"

"For making love to me. I practically begged him, but he was...unhappy."

Kate pulled into a parking place on the Plaza, the famous shopping center in Kansas City.

Before Susan got out of the car, however, she looked at Kate. "Does that sound right to you?"

"What do you mean?" Maggie demanded.

"Well, I've never heard a man apologize because he got to have sex. I mean, he'll apologize for almost anything to get to *have* sex, but not afterward."

"I imagine most women are better at it than I am."

"Oh, Maggie, don't be silly. Why wouldn't you be as good as any other woman?" Susan chided.

But Maggie had an answer for her.

"Because it was my first time."

Susan gulped and turned to Kate. "I don't have any experience in this area. Over to you, Kate."

Kate grinned. "Well, I wasn't very experienced myself, but Will never had any complaints. The more, um, experienced you become, the better you'll be, Maggie, so you've only got one way to go."

With a sigh, Maggie nodded. "And the first thing I have to do is get his attention."

"That I can handle," Susan promised.

The sisters had met at the diner that morning and left their cars there. When Kate pulled into the parking lot a few minutes before six, Maggie got out of the car and drew a shaky breath.

"You're going to knock him for a loop, Mary Margaret O'Connor," Kate said with a smile. "You look beautiful."

Susan smiled at her, nodding in agreement.

"Thank you both for...for all this," Maggie said with a trembling smile. "All this" consisted of a haircut that framed her face in a long pageboy with wispy bangs that drew attention to her hazel eyes; a short black skirt that hugged her trim hips and drew a man's eye to her shapely legs, clad in sheer stockings with slim black heels; a silk blouse, black with a jungle print, mostly green and gold, and a low-cut neck that hinted at a sexy décolleté; a gold-buckled belt that drew attention to her slim waist; delicate gold earrings that led a man's gaze to her slender neck; soft, natural-looking makeup that made her eyes appear huge, her lips ripe and kissable.

And to top it all off, a perfume that made her feel beautiful.

Her skin had been oiled and massaged, her nails shaped and polished, and she'd had a facial.

In the bags she carried to her car were several more outfits to wow her husband—the most daring of all, a peach-colored teddy that might arouse some interest at bedtime.

When she entered the house, coming in from the garage through the utility room to the kitchen, she self-consciously licked her lips, hoping her lipstick was still in place. "Josh?"

The kitchen was empty, but she heard steps coming down the stairs. Josh hit the kitchen door a minute later.

"You're back," he said as a greeting, Ginny in his arms. Then he came to an abrupt halt, his gaze widening in shock.

Remembering all the instructions from her sisters, she extended her arms and twirled around, then smiled at him. "Do you like my new look?"

He swallowed visibly, his gaze going up and down her. "Er, yeah. What's not to like?"

"How's Ginny?" Maggie asked as she picked up the packages she'd dropped to give Josh a complete look at her.

"Fine. Aren't you, angel? I didn't have any problems."

The pride in his voice made Maggie smile. Her new confidence amazed her and made everything easier. "Good. I'm glad you had a good day. Would you like to go out to eat? Kate has volunteered to baby-sit Ginny."

"Go out to eat?"

Her confidence suffered a little as he showed no enthusiasm. Kate had instructed her to make a reservation at a restaurant located on the Plaza, known for its steaks and its romantic aura.

"I...I wanted to celebrate. My new clothes and your new contract. Remember?"

"Yeah, I remember. That'd be great," he assured her, his voice husky.

She looked away, hoping to conceal her body's reaction to that huskiness. "Okay. I made reservations for seven."

"I'll hit the shower. You'll take care of Ginny?"

"Of course."

Less than an hour later they'd dropped Ginny off at Kate and Will's and driven the short distance to the Plaza. Once they were seated in the soft lighting at a table by a window that looked out on the lights of the Plaza, Maggie was at a loss. What now? They couldn't discuss their sex life in a restaurant.

"What's this new look going to cost me?" Josh asked, his gaze centering on the vee of her blouse.

Fighting the urge to place her hand over her exposed flesh, she said, "I paid for everything."

His head snapped up. "What?"

"I paid. I have a savings account and—"

"I'm your husband. *I'm* supposed to pay." His jaw

was squared, his voice inflexible. "You should've asked for a credit card. Damn, I should've already applied for some credit cards for you. And opened a checking account for you. I'll take care of everything. Tell me how much you spent today and I'll give you the money."

Maggie blinked at him several times. She didn't agree with his assumption that he should pay for her personal needs. But the fact that he intended to open accounts for her didn't sound like he planned a divorce.

"You...you intend to stay married to me?" she asked softly, staring at him.

He frowned and leaned forward, as if he wasn't quite sure what she'd said. The waiter chose that moment to appear at their table. Josh glared at him.

"Uh, you want me to come back later?"

"No, bring us two iced teas, salads with—what kind of dressing?" he asked Maggie.

"Ranch, please."

"Both ranch. Two rib-eye steaks, medium-well." He paused and hiked one eyebrow at Maggie in question and she nodded. "And two baked potatoes with everything on them."

"Except chives," Maggie added softly.

"Yeah," Josh agreed with a grin, taking the menu away from Maggie and handing both of them to the waiter. As soon as the man hurried away from their table, Josh leaned toward her. "What did you just say?"

"I asked if you planned to stay married to me."

He stared at her, either unable to believe what she

said or taking care with his response. "We've been
married a week tomorrow. Why would you think I
was ready to bail out already?"

"Because of Tuesday night."

Their superefficient waiter returned with two
glasses of iced tea and a basket of rolls with butter.
He offered them a smile, but Josh couldn't hold back
his glare. Damn, he wished they were home, alone.
Maggie was driving him crazy, making such bizarre
statements. Not to mention her beauty. He'd thought
her beautiful Tuesday night. And he'd been right. But
her looks tonight would attract every man within a
mile radius. Those who didn't know about her sweetness, her intelligence, her courage, her big heart.

He'd have to fight them off with a stick if he didn't
stay close to her.

Once the waiter stopped smiling at Maggie and
caught Josh's frown, he backed away from the table.

"Why would I want a divorce after Tuesday
night?" he asked quietly, his gaze intense.

Maggie picked up a roll and carefully buttered it,
avoiding his look. When he could stand it no longer,
he reached across the table to still the butter knife.

"Maggie?"

"I know s-sex wasn't part of what you offered."
She set the roll on her bread plate and tugged for him
to release her other hand.

"Hell, woman, you think I'm going to complain
about sleeping with you?"

She turned bright red, and Josh realized he'd spoken too loudly. Several customers at nearby tables were staring at them.

"Sorry," he whispered.

The waiter appeared again, two salads in his hands. Josh didn't bother to glare at him. He closed his eyes and waited until he heard his footsteps fading.

"Maggie, talk to me."

She took a bite of roll and chewed it until he thought he would grab her and drag her out of the restaurant. Finally, keeping her gaze glued to her salad, she said, "I understand, Josh. There's no need to feel bad about it. That's why I...I tried to change my appearance today."

Having thoroughly confused him, she picked up her fork and began eating her salad.

Josh shook his head, hoping to clear it enough to understand what Maggie had said. "You bought new clothes because I hurt you? Maggie, I swear I didn't intend to—"

"It's all right, Josh. I know you couldn't help it." She gave him such a sad look, he half rose out of his seat, intending to circle the table and take her in his arms. Until her alarmed look reminded him they were in a restaurant.

"Maggie, I swear to God it won't happen again."

Her look got even sadder, tears filling her eyes. "So...my new looks don't make a difference?"

Something was wrong. He didn't understand where this conversation was going. Cautiously he asked, "Why would your new clothes make a difference? You look great in them, of course, but—"

"I do?" A spark of pleasure lit her gaze. Then it disappeared. "But not enough to tempt you."

Josh rubbed his forehead. He was getting a headache. He drew a deep breath before saying, "Let's start over. What do you think happened Tuesday night?" He thought it was pretty obvious, but he had to get to the root of their misunderstanding. And that meant going back to Tuesday night.

"I...pleaded with you to make love to me. You did, but I...I didn't know how to please you, and you regretted it."

He couldn't believe her words. He felt his eyes bulge out as he stared at her. "*I* regretted it? Why would you think that?"

"You apologized."

The waiter appeared again, and Josh considered taking a swing at him. But it wasn't the boy's fault. And he had their dinners in his hands.

The waiter looked down at the table. "You haven't eaten your salads. Is there anything wrong with them?"

"No," Maggie said gently, smiling at him.

Josh felt a surge of jealousy go through him. He hadn't received such a nice smile since Tuesday night.

"Er, do you want me to bring these back later?" the waiter asked, lifting the two plates for clarification.

"No, leave them," Josh snapped.

The young man eased the plates onto the table, his gaze fixed on Josh. "Uh, if you need anything else, let me know."

He hurried away, leaving an awkward silence.

Josh struggled to gather control of himself, to explain to Maggie why he'd apologized. "I apologized because I hurt you."

"I know. It's not your fault you're not attracted to me." She kept her gaze on her salad and took another bite.

A lightbulb clicked on in Josh's head. When she'd said Josh had hurt her, she meant her feelings, because he wasn't attracted to her. Which, of course, was a ridiculous thought.

But a lot better one than he'd imagined.

"Maggie, I apologized because I hurt you *physically*." He waited for her gaze to lift.

She frowned. "I thought—I mean, I heard it always hurts the first time."

"Sweetheart, I didn't know you were a virgin. I could've been easier, more tender. I assumed—"

Her chest burned. "I didn't want to admit I wasn't experienced. I thought maybe you wouldn't know."

He reached across the table for her hand. "I didn't...until it was too late. And it killed me that I hadn't been more gentle."

The rising hope on her face lit a bonfire in Josh.

"You mean you didn't mind making—"

He stood and leaned over the table, pulling her to her feet, covering her lips with his, tasting her sweetness like a man starved for sustenance.

The sound of applause brought him to his senses, and he released Maggie, who sank down in her chair. With a wave to his audience and a grin that outshone the sun, he sat back down. "Maggie, I've wanted to make love to you since the night we first shared my bed. In fact, I was ready to fall to my knees and plead to make love to you again. That's why I wanted us to talk. I can't stand keeping my hands off you.''

"You...you like it?"

He groaned. "Like it? Maggie, I love you."

Maggie looked stunned for a moment, but then a smile lit her face.

"Oh, Josh, I love you. I want us to have a real marriage."

He couldn't stand it any longer. "Come on," he said, leaping to his feet.

"Where are we going?"

"Where do you think?" he asked her, grinning.

"But our food. We haven't eaten."

Josh turned around, nailing their waiter with a look that had the boy paling. Waving for him, Josh snapped when he arrived, "Bring the bill and box this food up to go."

"All of it?" the boy asked.

"Yeah, all of it. Here, here's my credit card. That will speed things up."

The boy gulped. "Yes, sir."

For the longest five minutes of his life, Josh stood with his arm around Maggie, whispering sweet words in her ears, waiting to escape to privacy.

Finally they reached the car. He zoomed out of the parking lot, even though Maggie cautioned him.

"Sweetheart, I've been suffering for three days, when you wouldn't even look at me. Now you're willing to make love and you want me to slow down?"

"No, I don't want you to slow down," she said with a seductive smile. "But I don't want you to get a ticket."

His eyebrows rose. "What happened to my innocent wife?"

"She spent some time in bed with a private investigator. And he showed her heaven," she said, her voice husky.

Josh groaned and pressed the accelerator harder.

After they reached home, in record time, they raced up the stairs. But when Maggie turned to go to her bedroom, Josh stopped her. "No, sweetheart, not tonight. We're going to the master bedroom, where a man and his wife belong."

She made no protest.

When they entered his room, he reached for the buttons on her blouse, and she returned the favor. When Josh discovered the sexy black bra and bikini panties she wore beneath her new clothes, he paused to admire her. "Sweetheart, wherever you did your shopping today, plan on going back and ordering some more things like this," he said, running a finger down the low curve of the bra.

"You like it?"

"I like it so much, we'd better hurry," he urged, slipping the straps down.

They fell on the bed after they'd removed their clothes and made up for the pain they'd suffered the past few days. True to his promises to himself, though, Josh was gentle, tender, caring of her inexperience.

And this time when they reached completion, he

gathered Maggie in his arms and held her close. "No tears, sweetheart?"

"Only those of happiness. I didn't do anything wrong?"

Josh chuckled. "Yes, you did. I didn't want to mention it, but..."

When he said nothing else, she struggled to sit up, but he wouldn't let her. "What? What did I do wrong?"

"You got me so excited I almost went too soon. Could you be less sexy next time?"

"Oh, you!" she protested, elbowing him.

"Ouch! Watch it woman. You might damage something," he teased.

"We wouldn't want to do that, because I'm going to keep you busy for a few years," she assured him, feeling more confident every moment.

"I don't think you'll get any complaints from me."

Epilogue

"Daddy!"

Two-year-old Ginny skidded into her daddy's home office, and Josh shoved back from the computer to reach out and catch her. "Hi, Ginny. Up from your nap?"

"Yes, and Mommy said come here."

He smiled at Ginny's precise words. She'd made amazing progress the past year, learning to walk—or maybe he should say run—and speak quite clearly.

"Okay, let's go find Mommy. Where is she?"

"She's on the bed."

Josh frowned. "On the bed?" He picked Ginny up and raced for the master bedroom. Maggie never took naps these days. She said she couldn't get comfortable.

"Maggie?" he called before he reached the door.

"In here," she called.

He found her sitting on the edge of the bed. "What's wrong?"

"Nothing. But it's time."

"Time?" he asked, puzzled. Then comprehension dawned and he stared at her bulging stomach. "*Time?* You mean the baby's coming?"

"Yes. I've called the doctor and—"

"It's time!" Josh exclaimed again.

"Get my suitcase, Josh. We need to drop Ginny off at Kate's. I called Angie and told her we'd be there in a few minutes."

"We don't have time for that! It's time!"

Maggie pushed herself off the bed. "Josh, get the suitcase."

Instead, he rushed to her side. "I'll carry you downstairs."

"Josh, I'll be okay. You carry Ginny and get my suitcase."

She waddled down the stairs, taking them one at a time, hoping her beloved husband would come to his senses. By the time she reached the bottom, he was right behind her.

"Are you sure we'll have time to drop Ginny off?"

"I promise we have plenty of time. The hospital is just on the other side of the Plaza. We're only fifteen minutes away."

"I want to see baby," said Ginny, reaching out a finger to touch Maggie's stomach.

"You'll have to wait a little while, sweetie. Soon your baby brother will be here. Daddy will bring you to the hospital as soon as he can." Maggie stopped and sagged against the wall, taking fast breaths as pain seized her.

"Maggie! Are you all right?" Josh demanded, dropping the suitcase and reaching for her.

"I'm fine...now. Let's go before I have another one."

They reached the hospital in plenty of time, after dropping Ginny off to play with Nathan. While Josh filled out all the forms, Maggie was disrobed and settled in the labor room.

He joined her as quickly as possible. "Are you all right? They made me fill out a lot of forms."

"I know. I'm fine. The doctor was in and said everything is moving along."

Though it didn't seem quick to Josh, Maggie's labor was relatively short. Their son, Joshua James McKinley, made his noisy appearance a little after seven that evening.

"Why's he still crying?" Josh asked with a frown.

"He's a hungry boy," the nurse chirped cheerfully.

"He's an impatient boy, just like his daddy," Maggie murmured with a smile.

"I just hope he's as lucky as his daddy," Josh whispered to Maggie before kissing her.

"You don't mind being a P.I. and a daddy, too?" she asked, knowing the answer already. Josh made sure she knew of his love every day.

"I can't imagine a better life, sweetheart."

Maggie knew the luckiest night of her life had been the one when Josh and Ginny walked into the diner.

"In fact," Josh continued, "I think being a private

investigator will come in handy in about ten or fifteen years.''

''Why?''

''Because Ginny and James, and any other babies we have, will be teenagers. But they won't be able to hide anything from their P.I. daddy.

''Perfect,'' Maggie said with a smile. And that described her life, she decided as she closed her eyes, with Josh, Ginny and baby James.

* * * * *

Beloved author **Judy Christenberry**
brings us an exciting new miniseries in

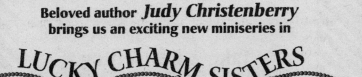

LUCKY CHARM SISTERS

Meet Kate in January 1999 in
MARRY ME, KATE (SR #1344)
He needed to avoid others meddling in his life. *She*
needed money to rebuild her father's dream. So William
Hardison and Kate O'Connor struck a bargain....

Join Maggie in February 1999 in
BABY IN HER ARMS (SR #1350)
Once Josh McKinney found his infant girl, he needed a
baby expert—quickly! But the more time Josh spent with
her, the more he wanted to make Maggie O'Connor his
real wife....

Don't miss Susan in March 1999 in
A RING FOR CINDERELLA (SR #1356)
The last thing Susan Greenwood expected was a marriage proposal! But cowboy Zack Lowery needed a
fiancée to fulfill his grandfather's dying wish....

A boss, a brain and a beauty. Three sisters marry for
convenience...but will they find love?

THE LUCKY CHARM SISTERS only from

Silhouette®

Available wherever Silhouette books are sold.

If you enjoyed what you just read,
then we've got an offer you can't resist!

Take 2 bestselling love stories FREE!

Plus get a FREE surprise gift!

Clip this page and mail it to Silhouette Reader Service™

IN U.S.A.	IN CANADA
3010 Walden Ave.	P.O. Box 609
P.O. Box 1867	Fort Erie, Ontario
Buffalo, N.Y. 14240-1867	L2A 5X3

YES! Please send me 2 free Silhouette Romance® novels and my free surprise gift. Then send me 6 brand-new novels every month, which I will receive months before they're available in stores. In the U.S.A., bill me at the bargain price of $2.90 plus 25¢ delivery per book and applicable sales tax, if any*. In Canada, bill me at the bargain price of $3.25 plus 25¢ delivery per book and applicable taxes**. That's the complete price and a savings of over 10% off the cover prices—what a great deal! I understand that accepting the 2 free books and gift places me under no obligation ever to buy any books. I can always return a shipment and cancel at any time. Even if I never buy another book from Silhouette, the 2 free books and gift are mine to keep forever. So why not take us up on our invitation. You'll be glad you did!

215 SEN CNE7
315 SEN CNE9

Name	(PLEASE PRINT)	
Address	Apt.#	
City	State/Prov.	Zip/Postal Code

* Terms and prices subject to change without notice. Sales tax applicable in N.Y.
** Canadian residents will be charged applicable provincial taxes and GST.
   All orders subject to approval. Offer limited to one per household.
   ® are registered trademarks of Harlequin Enterprises Limited.

SROM99   ©1998 Harlequin Enterprises Limited

This March Silhouette is proud to present

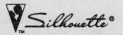

V Silhouette®

SENSATIONAL

MAGGIE SHAYNE
BARBARA BOSWELL
SUSAN MALLERY
MARIE FERRARELLA

This is a special collection of four complete novels for one low price, featuring a novel from each line: Silhouette Intimate Moments, Silhouette Desire, Silhouette Special Edition and Silhouette Romance.

Available at your favorite retail outlet.

V Silhouette®

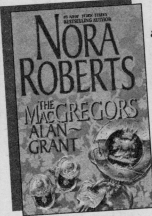
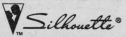

Based on the bestselling miniseries

FORTUNE'S Children™

A FORTUNE'S CHILDREN *Wedding:*
THE HOODWINKED BRIDE

by BARBARA BOSWELL

This March, the Fortune family discovers a twenty-six-year-old secret—beautiful Angelica Carroll *Fortune!* Kate Fortune hires Flynt Corrigan to protect the newest Fortune, and this jaded investigator soon finds this his most tantalizing—and tormenting—assignment to date....

Barbara Boswell's single title is just one of the captivating romances in Silhouette's exciting new miniseries, **Fortune's Children: The Brides,** featuring six special women who perpetuate a family legacy that is greater than mere riches!

Look for *The Honor Bound Groom,* by Jennifer Greene, when **Fortune's Children: The Brides** launches in Silhouette Desire in January 1999!

Available at your favorite retail outlet.

Silhouette®

Silhouette
ROMANCE™

COMING NEXT MONTH

#1354 HUSBAND FROM 9 TO 5—Susan Meier
Loving the Boss
For days, Molly Doyle had thought she was Mrs. Jack Cavanaugh, and Jack played along—then she got her memory back, and realized she was only his *secretary*. So how could she convince her bachelor boss to make their pretend marriage real?

#1355 CALLAGHAN'S BRIDE—Diana Palmer
Virgin Brides Anniversary/Long Tall Texans
Callaghan Hart exasperated temporary ranch cook Tess Brady by refusing to admit that the attraction they shared was more than just passion. Could Tess make Callaghan see she was his truelove bride before her time on the Hart Ranch ran out?

#1356 A RING FOR CINDERELLA—Judy Christenberry
The Lucky Charm Sisters
The last thing Susan Greenwood expected when she went into her family's diner was a marriage proposal! But cowboy Zack Lowery was in desperate need of a fiancée to fulfill his grandfather's dying wish. Still, she was astonished at the power of pretense when *acting* in love started to feel a lot like *being* in love!

#1357 TEXAS BRIDE—Kate Thomas
Charming lawyer Josh Walker had always wanted a child. So when the woman who saved him from a car wreck went into labor, he was eager to care for her and her son. Yet lazy days—and nights—together soon had Josh wanting to make Dani *his*…forever!

#1358 SOLDIER AND THE SOCIETY GIRL—Vivian Leiber
He's My Hero
Refined protocol specialist Chessy Banks Bailey had thirty days to transform rough 'n' rugged, true-grit soldier Derek McKenna into a polished spokesman. Her mission seemed quite impossible…until lessons in etiquette suddenly turned into lessons in love.…

#1359 SHERIFF TAKES A BRIDE—Gayle Kaye
Family Matters
Hallie Cates didn't pay much attention to the new sheriff in town—until Cam Osborne arrested her grandmother for moonshining! Hallie swore to prove her grandmother's innocence. But she was soon caught up in the strong, passionate arms of the law herself!